Chapter One

Months had flown by since K Rouga had the fortune of catching his twin brother slipping. Even though he was not actively in the streets looking for his brother he was always informed as to his whereabouts.

K Rouga never intended on shooting his little brother but things had gone from sugar to shit ever since their father died in a tragic car accident.

Being the eldest of the brothers K Rouga had inherited money from his father's life insurance policy, while his younger brother P Nouchy had not gotten so much as a dime from the policy.

Now, you may be asking yourself how this is possible when they were twin brothers, and normally being a twin meant that you had the same biological parent.

This phenomenon is called heteropaternal Superfecundation, which occurs when two of a woman's egg are fertilized by sperm from two different men.

Which meant that K Rouga and P Nouchy's mother, had been intimately involved with different men on or around the time just before or after having her menstrual cycle.

This was something that was very difficult to explain because their mother had grown up in a family that did not take any kind of sexual deviancy lightly.

So having multiple fathers in their lives would have been just as shameful as the act that led to the birth of the bipaternal twins.

Growing up in a household where their father Frederick was constantly in the streets, caused the brothers to have a strain on the brotherly bond that should have been natural from day one.

K Rouga and P Nouchy would always have arguments about whose father loved who more, and why neither of them chose to be an active part in their lives.

K Rouga said it was because P Nouchy was so ugly. While P Nouchy said it was because K Rouga was so dumb.

Either way, the lack of a constant male presence in their life, would one day become the catalyst for the destruction that the brothers would reap on themselves, and those who stood in their way.

The laws of karma had been biased against the brothers from the very beginning and would be upon them until the very end!

Meanwhile, Frederick didn't take too lightly to finding out that one of the children he thought was his, was indeed someone else's. Which made him feel like a fool and it challenged his manhood and everything that he thought he stood for.

This was why he didn't believe in marriage. Because Frederick had seen his mother get murdered by her husband in a blind fit of rage, and from that very moment on, he vowed to never love a woman enough to become permanently hinged to one woman.

So thus in fact, caused the streets to become the love of Fredericks life. It was the only thing that he truly understood. The only thing that would give him the kind of love that he wouldn't feel slighted in the least bit.

The only time he escaped from the streets was when he needed a little R and R. Rest and Recreation. In his mind Recreation meant Re-Creating as many babies as he could. After all, you only live once, so you might as well blast off every chance that you could.

Oftentimes, he allowed himself the luxury of staying the night at the homes of those lucky enough to share his romance.

But he never allowed himself to stay in one place for too long. Those who got comfortable in his line of work, ended up being comfortable laying in a wood grained casket, decked out in a old suit from the Brooks Brothers collection, with nothing but time on their hands to rest in eternal peace and hope to be reincarnated so they could have a new lease on life.

Frederick, who went by the name of "Bombay Blue", was a hustler in a long line of hustlers who carried the streets on their shoulders.

His hustling days had been days where he learned to maneuver the streets and camouflage to the surroundings so as to be invisible, all the while being able to roam freely in search of life's bounty. Which he referred to as the spoils of war.

Frederick was known to handle his business in the bedroom as well, which was why he always had his choice of whatever female companion he ended up with at night.

Out of all his encounters with his female "lady friends", he had only ended up with three children.

At least, those were the only three that he knew of. So if he had any other children, that was a thing for the government to deal with. That was why welfare was created. To be able for all the kids to be treated "Well" and "Fair" by the governing body of aristocrats.

Fredericks daughter Taraji, was born shortly after K Rouga and P Nouchy were born to Fredericks first baby mother Leslie.

The only fucked up fact was that Taraji was born to Leslie's best friend Felicity.

While both women shared a piece of the infamous "Bombay Blue", both of the women couldn't stand each other after their children were born.

Even though they grew up as best friends and they always had each other's back, they both felt betrayed with one another because they always vowed never to sleep with someone that the other one slept with.

Both women were stubborn and they knew that hell would literally "freeze over", before they made amends.

While Leslie was brown skinned, 5 foot 4, funny, witty,long black hair, that stopped at the bottom of her waistline, and a college graduate, Felicity was high yellow,6 foot even, short blonde hair, and a graduate of the "Hussla's" Academy.

Frederick was so mysterious in the way that he did business, that it was only right to keep his family life seperate as well. Solely for the well being of others. Felicity and Leslie in particular. He also tended to keep K Rouga and P Nouchy apart whenever he was around.

His actions had caused K Rouga and P Nouchy to never grow a bond close enough to create a love for each one another. Which was why K Rouga felt no remorse for what he was about to do.

"Stay right here baby, don't stray from this spot. You already know what I'm about to do. I've waited months to catch this bitch ass nigga slipping. I gotta hit him right now. Where it hurts", K Rouga said to his current flame who went by the name of Hershey.

"Do you baby. You already know I'm down to ride at all costs. You know it's all or nothing with me, and I'm ready to put it all on the line for you so that you know I'm serious. Go get that nigga", she replied.

K Rouga hopped off the front of the Amber whiskey/vivid black 2020 Harley Davidson low rider motorcycle and passed Hershey the helmet as he told her,

"Keep the bike on and keep ya hands on the throttle because I might come out of these projects wit a couple hunnid niggas on my trail like the wild wild west."

K Rouga was mentally striving to make light of the situation but he knew that this was no laughing matter. Once he did this, he knew things would become"worth dying for".

Simply because his twin brother wasn't a pushover in any way. But in a man's world, a man was defined by how much others"Respected" him. And K Rouga was tired of the disrespect that P Nouchy displayed openly. Things were about to change.

"I got you. Just get back safely baby." Hershey said before K Rouga disappeared in the belly of the projects "Ironically" named as the "Twin" towers.

(Meanwhile.......Somewhere in the projects)

P Nouchy stood in the mirror as he looked at the creases that lined his features and contemplated his financial situation. Having a father like Frederick had paid off, because he had taught him how to keep things lined up and keep his finances in order.

It wasn't really about the money. It was what to "do" with the money. He was caught up in a bind because he wanted to invest his last $150,000 into purchasing a few kilos of that white girl he referred to as "Red Velvet", or continue to pay for his mother's healthcare, who was in the hospital battling Covid19.

In his book, he would go broke rather than to allow the health of his mother to deteriorate due to any negligence on his part. On the flip side of a fucked up coin,P Nouchy would be damned if he spent all his money on Felicity's healthcare and ended up broke at the end of the day.

That wasn't an option. Which left him with the option to just take half of the $150k and invest, and hope that he could turn milk into butter that would bring forth good tidings for all.

Yeah, that was what he was going to do. He had made arrangements earlier in the day to meet with his right hand man named Fred. How ironic to have a right hand man whose name happened to be the name of his father.

Interrupted by his Note 11 vibrating on his hip, P Nouchy grabbed the phone and swiped the indicator to answer the call,

"Speak". He answered.

"What up boss, I'm just hitting you to let you know that your brother is in the projects and he looks to be headed your way. Do you want us to stop him?"

"Nah. Let him move freely. Just make sure that he ain't carrying a piece".

"Aight hold up, let me scan him."

P Nouchy immediately went to the safe that was located in the master bedroom of his apartment and retrieved a semi automatic pistol that was untraceable.

It wasn't as if he was expecting trouble from his brother, but he wanted to be sure that it wasn't any funny business going on. P Nouchy wasn't in the mood for the bullshit that had surrounded the family lately.

Ever since the death of Frederick, the family was divided. Yet, P Nouchy couldn't understand why. Something wasn't right. Yet, he couldn't grasp the hidden meaning that eluded him.

"Boss?"

"Speak."

"He is carrying a weapon. The thermal imaging system picked up a distinct shape along the left side of his denim jeans that he is wearing. Do you want us to disarm him before he reaches you?"

"No, I'm going to speak to him outside anyway. I have a feeling that this isn't a social visit. Put the others on point but let them know that I don't want anybody to use their weapon unless I order so. Let me see what this nigga talking about."

"Ok boss I got u."

P Nouchy hung up the phone and retrieved his bulletproof vest. After putting it on and placing a Black Dolce and Gabbana sweatshirt that read "I am greatness,"over it, he was ready to go.

He spoke into the hooded end and said"I'm on the move."

"Ok boss I see you and I got you covered. What else do you need done?"

"Nothing. I got this."

"Say no more boss. I have eyes on the back of you. You just worry about the front."

P Nouchy walked past the crowded end of the Twin Towers projects. The projects were twin apartment complexes that were adjoined to one another so that the whole building was connected. The projects had a small amusement park for the children which was now empty due to the early hours that the darkness settled in.

The projects were gang infested with members of the infamous"Bloods"gang. Located on 184th Street in the East section of the Bronx, it was only right that the inhabitants of the geographic location would be "Bloods".

That was easy to see because of the history of O.G MACK, who caught his first body right around the corner on 183rd Street and Valentine Avenue, which was also part of Bloods history due to a famous "Valentine's Day Massacre", which earned the street name Valentine Avenue, which also became a chapter of a Blood Set called The Valentine's Bloods.

So caught up in his stroll down memory lane, P Nouchy didn't hear his brother creep up behind him and place the barrel of a gun to the back of his neck.

He thought to himself"So much for his security detail watching his back". Not only was he mad at himself for getting caught slipping, he was mad at Rozay, for allowing his brother to get all the way up on him and not say shit.

"Shit". He said under his breath. Before he continued,"To what do I owe the pleasure of cold steel on my neck?"

K Rouga was tempted to put a slug in his brain off the top. But he wanted to look in the eyes of his brother and find peace for what he was going to do. He nudged his brother in the head as he told him,

"It's always a pleasure to get rid of tainted blood. Sorta like a blood transfusion. Dialysis. Or in hood language it would be pronounced as DIE-I'LL-ASSIST. Meaning I'll help your bitch ass die!!! What you think about that lil nigga?"

P Nouchy couldn't help but laugh inside at his brother's attempt to make a joke. He was always the goofy one in the family and it had led to them getting into numerous altercations where P Nouchy would always have to come to the rescue and save his brother from getting his ass kicked.

"You know, I'm not afraid of you or death. I've been expecting you for a long time. Since pops died, I've noticed the hostility in your voice, actions, and it's crazy when I think about it. So all I wanna know is why? Why do you wanna end my reign as King? It ain't like you will ever get my throne."

"Funny... Really funny.. How dare you make jokes when I have a gun pointed at your head".

"You might have a gun, but you don't have the balls. Just like my bitch. You've always been a bitch. You always looked for me to come save the fucking day when niggas was ready to beat yo ass. So don't take today as the day to start getting tough. Ha ha ha ha ha", P Nouchy started laughing until.....

"Click Clack". K Rouga cocked back the hammer on the 9 millimeter Smith and Wesson and pressed it to the dome of his brother.

"Turn yo punk ass around muhfucka and let me look in your eyes while I squeeze off. Treat you how I treat my bitches".

"Drop the gun bro, it don't even have to be like this. Word."

K Rouga looked at his brother and felt nothing but hatred for him. He wanted nothing but to end his life and be done with it forever. He paused for a second before continuing,

"You think shit sweet Lil bra?" K Rouga asked his brother, With a look of pure determination and pure disgust in his eyes as his heart was turning cold. His mind was calculating his odds.

P Nouchy looked in his brother's face and was overcome with rage. He continued to ponder on his words as he spoke,

"Ain't shit sweet but the eternal rest that all of us is destined. Seems like you think shit is sweet cause you got a gun in my face like you really bout that Life. Like you really built like that. The only reason you live is because I allow you to live. You aren't enough of a threat for me to want you dead.

Especially not over the petty change you stole from me. Even when daddy gave yo dumb ass all the money on his life insurance policy. That wasn't good enough for you. You wanted my money. Muhfuckas like you is only loyal to the crabs in the barrel.

And even then, y'all bring everybody down with you. That's why it wouldn't bother me if you kill me. I know you would be dead before you take another step".

Looking over at his brother, P Nouchy no longer felt emotion towards him. For what it was worth, K Rouga was now a dead man walking.

His mind raced back to so many occasions where he had come to the aid of his brother. Even though he was the younger sibling by 5 minutes, he was the one that the streets respected more.

Simply because of his no holds barred attitude, when it came to dealing with people who crossed lines and boundaries that had been established since the beginning of mankind.

Which brought P Nouchy to the question of what was the intentions of K Rouga to be so brazen as to pull a gun on him.

"We can take him out boss. Just give us the orders." The voice of Rozay came through the earpiece that was hooked up to a special spot sewn on the majority of the upper body garments that P Nouchy wore on a regular basis. This enabled P Nouchy to always be in the loop when it came down to his protection detail.

The majority of the hoodies that P Nouchy wore came from a company called the "Hoody Buddy".

Their sweatshirts came with earbuds incorporated in them through the strings that pulled the hoodie tight. Everytime he wore a sweatshirt he plugged his earbuds into the Note 11 phone so that he was able to have both his hands free at any moment. Every moment. Knowing that all it took was a moment to slip and that moment would cause a casket to dip.

P Nouchy smiled to himself as he spoke under his breath and told Rozay to stand down. Funny as it seemed, even before the encounter with his brother P Nouchy knew what time it was. It was always, only a matter of time before jealousy reared it's nasty invocations in the minds of mere mortals.

It reminded Nouchy of the early day prophecies which revealed that in the end times of the world, family ties would be reduced to ashes in a fire. There would be nothing that would stop families from victimizing, hurting, and killing each other. All in the name of maintaining self worth and value. It truly was a,"Dog eat Dog" world. But when it came down to fighting against ignorance, Nouchy believed in giving people the benefit of the doubt.

It had become natural for people to kill and murder each other, hurt and maim one another, steal and cheat one another, these there was no code of conduct to live by. Because you have 2 options. Either you are the victim, or you are the predator.

Either you are the Lion or you are the Sheep. There is no way of mediating the terms where things are 50/50. Where things are equal for the progression of everyone.

Someone has to be the loser and someone has to be the winner. It's a" winner take all" kind of world. Which was why Nouchy never understood the value of life. To lose was to die. To win was to live to see another day in a fucked up society that spared nobody. Not even the innocent babies of the world. In other words "ANYBODY CAN GET IT".

"I copy that boss, but he has the jump on you right now, are you sure you want us to stand down?" Rozay spoke into the earpiece as he crept up behind K Rouga with his suppressed Russian Makarov, itching to pull the trigger.

Nouchy looked at K Rouga and saw a defiant look in his eyes that gave him the impression of something being imminent, but he still gave the order to stand down. He wanted his brother to give him reason to shed his blood. He would not justify the blood of his brother being shed without provocation. Eye 4 An Eye was not only a statement. It was a Creed that he lived by.

"Who the fuck you talking to stupid nigga?" Rouga asked Nouchy.

"Oh, I'm just talking to God. We was trying to figure out if we wanted to die today or not. You know I'm surrounded by the spirit of our father. He's been recruiting Angels and other spirits that protect me and my best interests. Which leaves me to ask you, are you just gonna stand there with that gun, or are you gonna make me a believer like a New Age Christian, cause right now I'm a atheist. And personally, YOU a real bitch ass nigga if you don't kill me sucka!!!

K Rouga ignored the comment as he surveyed his surroundings. His 2nd sense was tingling and he felt like this wouldn't be a good time to take a stand against his brother. Even though this was the closest that he had ever been to catching his brother alone, he wasn't sure that he was in fact, alone.

He spoke up,"You know something, I used to respect you. But now, I don't respect you. I hate you for what you have become. You are the reason your mother is in the hospital now. I would kill you right now but that would kill her in the process. So even though you think I'm a coward, that shows how much you really know about me. You are so caught up in your delusions that you will die an idiots death. For always underestimating people. Pops always told us that" looks can be deceiving".

In the next instant K Rouga shifted the 9 millimeter and fired 3 times in the direction of his little brother.

"Boom!!! Boom!!! Boom!!!"

Nouchy was aware that he had been shot but didn't realize that he had fallen to the ground until he touched the pavement. He had actually felt the hot slugs as they entered his legs, and although he didn't want to, had no choice but to fall to the ground as the bullets stripped him of the choice to remain standing.

Except, he didn't remember falling. Around him, he heard suppressed fire from the Makarov that Rozay was letting off in the direction of his fleeing brother.

"Don't shoot him Rozay", he told him with as much strength as he could muster.

"Why not boss?" He asked as he went off in the direction of where he had last seen K Rouga.

"Because the cops will be here in any minutes and I need you to get me to the crib. You know I need to get off the block. These muhfuckas is on neighborhood watch out this bitch. Get your ass back here pronto!!!".

(Meanwhile)

K Rouga ran back the way he came. Just barely escaping the barrage of bullets that had come from an unknown source, he knew that he was lucky to escape with his life. But he knew that whatever happened next, he had to be real careful or he would die.

When he got back to the motorcycle he jumped on and told Hershey to go. She hesitated and said,"How did it go babes"?

"I shot that muhfucka. Now let's get up out this area. I hate the fucking smell of the projects. Drop me off at A Rich spot".

" I cooked you some food since you didn't come home last night. I thought you would at least come home with me and dig this pussy out the frame before you left to handle your business baby". She told him.

"I wouldn't mind doing all that baby, but in case you didn't hear me the first time, I shot my brother. I don't know if you are just horny as hell, but you know the deal behind that. You know the ramifications behind some shit like that. I need to hole up and rethink my next move."

Hershey revved up the bike and burned rubber as she sped off in the direction of the George Washington bridge. She didn't even reply to K Rouga as she knew that he wouldn't be able to hear her anyway due to the fact that she was going 85 miles per hour.

She focused on the road and the ride ahead as she thought to herself, "Girl I hope you know what you doing cause the body count will not hesitate to add you to it"!!!

Some things were better left unsaid when it came to her dealings with K Rouga. The sex was blazing and he was loyal to her when they were "officially" a couple.

There was nothing that she would not do for him. In any way shape or form. She would take a bullet for him if need be. But it was his stubbornness and the fact that he constantly disregarded her opinion in matters of life and death, that took a toll on her.

She wasn't always certain that he had "THEIR" best interests at heart. Because he didn't care about some of the things he did. And it was that reckless abandon that made her scared for her own safety and she didn't know if she could do this too much longer.

She would not sacrifice her life because K Rouga wanted to prove to others that he was something that in essence he really wasn't. Which was why she vowed NEVER to be caught in the current when the sharks came for Blood!!!!!!!!!

Chapter Two

After the incident with Rouga, Nouchy decided to move his operations to his more secure home in Hoboken, New Jersey. The gunshot wounds that he had sustained as a result of the actions of Rouga had left him with limited mobility in his right leg where two bullets had eaten into the upper part of his thigh.

The other bullet had grazed his right kneecap just enough to add a pinch of irritation to the already somber mood that had enveloped him as he thought of ways to extract revenge.

At first, the sight of all the blood streaming from his wounds made him feel that it was a serious injury. But, after a thorough inspection by the doctor who was on call, who also happened to be a close friend of his, he had been comfortable enough to wrap both areas with a torniquet until he could get to the condo in New Jersey.

He couldn't help but to start laughing to himself as he replayed his homegirls reaction to seeing him bloodied up.

"What the fuck you done did, better yet, who the fuck did this to you so I can go squeeze a whole clip at that muhfucka.!!! Damn honey, seem like you find trouble or trouble finds you every other week. You better not let grandma find out about this shit, cause you know it'll give her a damn reason to preach to yo ass."

Nouchy started to laugh, but was instantly shut down from the pain in his body. He could barely get his words out as he responded,

"Hey, calm the fuck down lil whodie. Seems like you preaching already. All grandma gotta do is sing the damn music. Shut yo ass up and give me medical attention before I bleed the fuck out in this bitch. I called my doctor, not my damn homegirl. So turn the homegirl switch off for a minute and let me get some help over here. You know I'ma tell you what happened. So you can sell it to TMZ. You know them bitches love to gossip."

TMZ was a reference to the other three homegirls that his homegirl hung out with on a daily basis. Tianna, Mercury, and Zoe. All three of them went to pre-med school together and it was through their dedication, determination, and devotion, that they survived the onslaught that all medical students endure.

From test and test, to the hands on tests, to the internships at Montefiore Hospital in the Bronx, they had held firm in their convictions and made sure to see their dreams through as realities.

"Boy shut the hell up and be still while I figure out if I'ma help you or let you die. If you be nice to me I'll give you a shot of that "Morphine Power Rangers" to numb that pain you feeling. You know you a lil wimp anyway."

"You win sis. You've been getting off on me since we were young. But you can keep the Morphine, I got a bottle of Ciroc. Fix me up a couple martinis and pop a pain pill. Time to get on Micheal Jackson level. See what he saw before he clocked out."

"Brvvvvv!!!! Brvvvvv!!!!Brvvvvv!!!Brvvvvv!!!"

The cell phone in Nouchy's pocket began to vibrate as his homegirl Keke stripped off her rubber gloves.

"Answer the phone nigga. You know you want to. If I wasn't in here you would be on the phone with them bitches you got. Gold digging pirates!!! Hmmmmph!!!"

Nouchy looked at his homegirl and shook his head as he activated the answer button on the Note 11 and spoke into the receiver.

"Speak."

"I have everything ready to go boss." Rozay told him before continuing," I've made a few calls as you requested and I told Nunu to get the other squad together and they will be meeting up at the second location. Once they are there do you want them to come to New Jersey or will you let Nunu inform them?"

Nouchy paused for a second and allowed himself to gather his thoughts before responding to his First in command.

"Call Nunu again and tell him to meet me in Hoboken. I'm on my way up there right now. Call S.A. and let him know that I have a job for him to do and I want him to meet me in Yonkers at the horsetrack on Wednesday. Tell Rapper to get that bread from the stash and cop that work on behalf of the Empire. Tell him to give the plug 10 extra grand just for my absence. You can give them this number right here because I'm going to throw this phone away later on today. Matter fact, do you still have that connect at Verizon?"

"Yeah boss, I still rocks wit Scooby. She official !"

"Ok. Tell Scooby that I need a whole shipment of them new Galaxy phones. The ones that don't cut off if you drop them in the water. Like my phone I have now. And tell her that I want a few flip phones as well. Let me know what the ticket is and holla back at me. Okay?"

"Anything else boss?"

"Nothing for right now. However, I'd like to take this moment to tell you that I appreciate your quickness earlier today. Although you were late on the draw, you still were there when it counted. I don't know what happened to the other two knuckleheads who were supposed to be on post. We'll handle that like a door frame when I get well. I know where your loyalty lies."

He paused for a second before continuing.

"Don't mistake my hesitance of not harming my brother as a sign of weakness. Everything happens for a reason. And everything comes full circle in due time. Now is not the time to wage war on my brother. Felicity is currently on her death bed. The last thing I want her to leave this world with, is the memory of a family that was divided. Even if its true that what she doesn't know won't hurt her. I'm willing to wear these bullet wounds as a testament, to her constant sacrifices in raising me right. If and when she exits this world, only then will I be able to extract revenge. Even though I don't honestly want to hurt my brother, it's a must. Only because he shed my blood. I gave that imbecile everything that he never had. Money. Power. Respect. Fame. His own crew doesn't respect him. The nerve of this fool to even take it there with me. It hurts me to my core, but I gotta go numb. No feelings. No emotions. Just do it how it needs to be done. It is what it is. Just as long as when it's over with, everybody knows that I'm still in charge. I built this Empire. This ain't no TV show. It's real life. Like the old saying goes, it's an eye for an eye. He will regret this day before he dies. I will make sure of it!"

"Say no more boss. You know I'm here for you all day everyday!"

"Team Empire!!!" Nouchy exclaimed.

"Is the only Empire that matters!!" Rozay responded before he hung up the phone and went off to handle the next part of the mission at hand.

Nouchy smiled to himself as he knew what would eventually come. Rozay was certified and he was one of his trusted soldiers. His level of ruthlessness was matched to none. And before it was all said and done, there would be more bodies than the coroner would be able to keep up with. But if this is what K Rouga wanted, he would give it to him. Ten times over.

"McClain you have a visit. Get ready to go out with the next movement," Officer Moralez said as she bent over to tie her shoes, before continuing on her rounds in the dormitory that Spencer"Malachi"McClain was housed in.

Spencer McClain was an illegitimate son of Frederick. Meaning, although Frederick was not the biological father of Spencer, he had provided for Spencer his whole life.

Frederick was the only father figure that was around for Spencer. Even though the visits came far and between, there was always money on the family account at the corner store, and they're was always food on the table. More than enough to satiate the taste buds of "Malachi" as he was known only by Frederick and his family.

Growing up with little assistance, (hands on treatment), as his mother described, Malachi was antisocial and chose to live in the shadows, while always seeming to find trouble at the end of every road.

His first encounter with violence came at the hands of the school's hallway monitor, who felt the need to display his machoism in front of a couple of girls who Malachi had a crush on. Known for his racist ways, the hallway monitor was quick to assume that the skinny little black kid was just like all of the other " Puppy Monkey Babies" that he had handled and put in their place.

Malachi had heard about the ways of the hallway monitor whose name was "David". However, he had many encounters with David but none of those encounters were to the extent where there was any confirmation to the rumors that circulated the school . So Malachi never felt afraid of David or anyone else.

Frederick had always taught Malachi to preserve his anger and always be humble in his ways. The moments that Frederick shared with Malachi, were always learning moments. Moments that defined character within. Malachi taught that a bad attitude was like a flat tire.

You wouldn't go anywhere until you changed it. That element of wisdom had been a model for the way Malachi lived. Even though he didn't have a father, he had hope and purpose and a sense of direction for his life. If only things were that simple.....

Malachi had just been excused to use the bathroom after a long two hours of taking the yearly mandatory exam that determined whether you would be graduated to the next grade or left behind.

His thoughts were only focused on draining the hot liquid from his bowels that made his balls throb with pain. His focus was so off target that he wasn't paying attention to where he was headed and as he rounded the corner to the boys restroom, he plowed headfirst into the arms of an already enraged David.

David had been upset because his mother had found his father's stash of child pornography on their computer and had turned him in to the authorities. She couldn't stand the fact that there was a monster living under her roof.

Because of her childhood, she hated any man who had a fetish for children. Even if it was a man that she had vowed to love for better or worse. Fuck that shit!!! The worse was enough to get him a new address as far as she was concerned.

David was carrying the books for a pretty black girl named Ebony. Even though he hated the black boys, he had a thing for all girls. No matter the color or the weight or whether or not she was dumb as a bag of rocks or bright as a Thomas Edison lightbulb.

When Malachi exploded into David and all of the books fell from his hands, his anger got the best of him and his temper exploded as he grabbed Malachi and shoved him against a locker.

"Watch where the fuck you going you Puppy Monkey Baby. You know you could get a beatdown for messing with the wrong person. Now PICK UP ALL OF THOSE

BOOKS AND GIVE THEM TO ME!!! RIGHT NOW NIGGER!!" he yelled at Malachi.

Malachi was always a wisecrack when it came to any situation he was faced with. So his first thought was to respond with,"You need to watch where you park that dumptruck that's illegally parked in your mouth. No wonder all you do is talk shit. Whewwwww!!!

He pulled out his cell phone and made believe that he was calling someone on the phone before he continued,

"Yeah... Hello???..... Yes..... I would like to place an order for a tow truck..... Yeah.... Well, it's a dumptruck parked illegally and it's blocking the necessary oxygen from going to my brain.... Yeah... The address??.... Oh ok... It's, Please come quick, David's shitty mouth drive, Save a nigga from deaths door, 11269..... Ok... Thank you".

He hung up and told David, "Towtrucks on the way to fix that problem you have. Now let's see about these books"....

As he bent down to pick up the books he noticed for the first time, the two girls standing behind David. Had he known that they were there in the first place, he would have kept the wisecrack going. But he really did have to use the bathroom with an intensity that was overriding his comedian side. So he simply said,"Hello Ebony, Hello Sasha", and went to do what he was doing.

David was enraged at being joked on and he heard the sniffles and giggles of the girls behind him and that turned the button on in his mind that was set to, "full ass kicking mode" as he grabbed Malachi's head and brought his knee to meet it with the force of a long punter kicking a football.

Thud!!! Smack!!!! As knee connected with impact, Malachi felt the blinding pain enter his head, a second after the blow from David.

"Arrrrrrrggggghhhhhh", he screamed as he scrambled to get away from the pain.

"Don't you run now you little punk. Come your black nigger ass back here. Let me show you what it's like to be towed by a truck. Ain't that what you called for?!!! A Towtruck?? Well here I am nigger boy!!!"

As Malachi heard the words nigger boy, he was overcome with anger. His pain that he felt, did not even compare to the pain that his ancestors had suffered at the hands of people like David. People who had no care in the world for those who were not of the same color skin that they were.

So they chose to display mannerisms that forced those underneath them (as they called it), to bow down or to be put to death by any method thought of.

Ebony quickly saw the direction that this could head in, and she quickly ran to David and begged him to take it easy on Malachi.

"Please David, don't hurt him, he was just joking with you. Let him pick up the books so we can go."

Her words fell on deaf ears. All David felt was Ebony trying to pull him from his"Catch of the day", and he turned around and smacked Ebony across the face. SMACK!!!

Mind your business you nigger whore. You're just like that black carcass right here. I'll take care of you after I roast this nigger pig..."

Malachi saw the way that Ebony went down and went after David with a vengeance that he didn't know he possessed. It was as if the souls of Nat Turner, Sojourner Truth, Harriet Tubman, Malcolm X, and Dr Martin Luther King Jr, jumped into his body all at once and he found the strength to fight the fight that he was destined to fight.

"Grrrrowwwwwwwlllllllllll", David heard the noise before he felt the pain in the back of his head from where Malachi sucker punched him.

Both boys continued to battle with each other as David landed a nice jab to the chin of Malachi, and followed the jab with a powerful punch to the gut of Malachi that blew the air out of him.

"Fight back Malachi!!!" Ebony screamed as she ran up to slap the shit out of David in order to give Malachi time to get right.

SLAP!!!!!

"Get your white hands off of him. You big bully. Hit me cracker. HIT ME!!!

Ebony continued to barrage David until he turned his attention towards her.

"You want me to hit you bitch? Come here!!!" He said as she began walking backwards at the same time Malachi struggled to his feet.

Malachi knew that he had to do something drastic in order to get this fight to end asap. He then remembered something that Frederick had told him and decided to put it to use in order to see what it would do to a sick fuck like David.

As David grew nearer to Ebony, Malachi rushed forward and grabbed the back of his shirt and turned him around with the force of a twister and a tornado.

"Come here mothafucka!!! Hmmph!!! Hmmph!!" He said as he hit David in the solar plexus and in the stomach. As David began to double over from the shortness of breath that he was experiencing, Malachi picked him up with a ferocious uppercut to the top of his face. Just above the bridge of his nose.

"Get yo bitch ass crackerjack. As Davids head came up level with Malachi, Malachi came off of his back foot with a forward thrust and whipped his head and smashed it into his nose.

"Crunch!!!!!" he heard the sound of bone crunching as David let out a blood-curdling scream...

"Aaaaaaaarrrrgghhh..Owwwwwwwww...Pbbbbbb"

"Don't scream now pussy,get your ass on the floor and pick those books up and give them to me before I fuck your ass up some more. Do it white boy!!!!"

With all the commotion going on in the hallway, there was now a crowd of onlookers who had crowded the hallway to witness the scene. Many had been there for the last part of the fight but a lot of them showed up just in time to see the defeat in the eyes of David.

There was no mistaking who had done what to whom, and even though both fighters were bloody and bruised beyond comparison the crowd was with Malachi on this day. Alot of victims of David had taken the opportunity to take pictures of the bruised boy as he gathered up all of the books one by one and placed them in the hands of Malachi.

As the last book was gathered and placed in the hand of Malachi,he grasped the shirt of his enemy and spoke softly in his ear so as not to be overheard by the other kids as he spoke.

"Today is the last day that you are a hall monitor. Take your badge and give it to the principal and tell her you quit. Today is the last day you bully any of my black brothers and sisters. Today is the last day that you call my people out of their name, because today is the last day that I will allow you to mess with my people. Today is the last day you will speak unless spoken to. Because if you do I will find you and I will beat your ass every day of the school semester until you drop the hell out, or you kill yourself, do I make myself clear?"

Even though his pride was wounded, he knew the sound of sincerity in a person's words from all the times his father told him" I'm going to beat your ass", so David had no choice but to say yes.

Malachi wanted to humiliate him further, but he let everything go because he had made his point. Frederick had instilled in him the ferociousness of the moment, and after seizing victory,being able to be cordial and resume composure and humility.

As he began to walk away he heard chants of "Ma-la-chi, Ma-la-chi ,Ma,la,chi", and he knew at that moment that he was destined to be the beacon of hope for so many others. So that had been his outlook on life until the day that he had committed a grave sin and murdered his best friend while defending the honor of another friend.

Convicted of murder at the age of 19 he was sentenced to 45 years, that was 18 years ago. He had grown up in the system in an environment where there was no love given, no love lost, no love period.

Just cold and callous individuals looking to gain something from someone for nothing.

The hardest thing that Malachi had to experience was leaving his younger siblings behind while he went off to jail. Even though Frederick wasn't his biological father, he had shown him so much love over the years, that he was around when Frederick had children with Felicity and Leslie.

Malichi was quick to want to be a part of their upbringing. He struggled to teach them the ropes, knowing how cold,calculative, manipulative, persuasive, and conniving, the streets could be.

He assured them that their only option at being respected was to demand respect at all costs. In the end,a good person had died in order for that respect to be kept.

Not only did he demand respect for himself he demanded respect for the whole clan, his inner circle, and his neighborhood.

More than a role model to the youth and his neighborhood many people were devastated at the charges that landed him in prison.

However that did not stop the ongoing support that he had gotten from so many people. From mail, money orders, pictures and other memorabilia, it kept him grounded as he sought to find evidence in his case that warranted a new trial, and or vacation, of the current sentence imposed by the state.

"I wonder who's coming to see me on a bright Saturday morning,"he told his roommate Pride.

"Whoever it is, beat the count being cleared. They must have slept in the damn parking lot all night to be up here this early. Ha,ha,ha. Shiddddd it gotta be important bro. You might want to put your boots on and lace them up in case you need to kick some ass." Pride told him.

"Nah I doubt I'll have to smack a negro today. Last fight I had was a couple years ago. I'm not looking to fight anytime soon", Malachi said as he got his fresh visit uniform out from under his mattress.

He paused before looking over the uniform to make sure that it still met his standard of crispiness. It had to be a crispy uniform. Crispy was a term that was made up by the inmates to describe anything brand new in the prison system.

Malachi put on the pants first and then remarked to himself, "Man I'm still a fly ass brother!!"

Pride looked at him and said, "You bout as fly as that damn mosquito carrying that damn zika virus Nigga, or as fly as a plane that's low on gas.. Ha ha ha. You have no juice. I can't knock you tho, you got that bitch Moralez on your jock strap roomie,"Pride told him.

"Must you defoul the atmosphere with ignorant language of an idiot early in the morning, at let's see....."

Malichi said as he rotated his wrist so he could read the time.

"Eight, twenty three,thirty five Am. "he said.

"Eight what?!! replied Pride.

"Hours, minutes,and seconds fool."

"Whatever Mr science Guy."

"You know better than to call ladies bitches, at least that's a part of science in your mathematics. Come on big bro you know better."

"Enough said. Don't go Malcolm X on me just yet, save that for your visit. I'm out!" Pride said as he kicked the door open and began to leave the room to give his roommate some privacy.

"Don't run now black man, this ain't the days of slavery. Come back here and let me plant some seeds in the mental field for you. Ha,ha,ha."

Malachi finished getting ready for visit and went to get a pass for visit. He had to wait on the departure of the other people going to visit, so that they could all go at once, as the officers on duty only did one visit movement at a time every 20 minutes.

Going down the sidewalk he saluted a few fellow brothers of the drill team that he was involved in. The drill team was a group of individuals who were drawn to the idea of starting a military-style barracks dorm.

The whole idea was brought forth as the solution to ending some of the violence around the whole compound that he was residing at.

Dr. Martin Luther King Jr. once said, "The ultimate measure of a man is not where he stands in moments of comfort and convenience, but where he stands in times of challenge and controversy!'

After speaking to a few people he made his way to the visitation room and checked his coat and ID at the desk before he went into the visitation room.

As he made his way to the section that his table was at, he scanned the room to see who was here to see him.

As his eyes settled on the familiar face of his younger brother K Rouga, the expression on his face told Malachi that something was bothering him, but there was no indication on his face about whether it was good news or bad news.

This was what Malachi referred to as going in blind. Certain situations called for certain reactions, and methods of resolving the situation. Malachi was good at observation and recognition of behavioral patterns,as he had spent two years in the Marines as part of the enlisted branch of Marines stationed at Parish island.

His job consisted of studying his peers and recognizing signs of stress, discomfort, insomnia,paranoia, and other signs of emotional instability. He got so good at recognizing people, that he used his skills on his senior officers in order to manipulate planned activities, and planned training sessions.

His peers called him professor because of his demeanor and attitude. The senior officers commended him on his growth and gave him recommendations for him to become a junior commissioned officer.

But a weekend of leave from the United States Marine corps had ended up with Malachi in handcuffs and his dreams of being enlisted at the top brass of the Marines,put on hold.

Snapping out of the daydream, Malachi approached the table amidst glances and smiles, winks from admirers sizing him up and down. He shrugged it off and casually strolled to the table.

He looked up and down at his brother and sized him up and came up with an opinionated summary of his brother's size.

"You've been working out or you've been lifting a lot of big girls out there..." he told K Rouga as he embraced his brother with the soliditary greeting of a dap and a hug.

He could feel his brother tense up as he hugged him and a subtle attempt at a false laugh did not go unnoticed by Malachi.

"Yeah big bro, I've been getting it in. You left a lot of turkeys out there that needed to be plucked. So I'm holding you down you know it's only so much exercising a nigga can do,but that turkey plucking job gets my condition right where it needs to be.

Malachi looked his brother up and down one more time before continuing, "More or less,more or less. Have a seat young one. Don't tell me that you came all this way to stand up and look at me. What's on your mind?"

"You hungry bro, you want something out of the vending machine? I had got this key card and put $35 on it so you could get some decent grub."

"Why are you so quick to change the subject? I'll let you know what I want in a minute after we have caught up a little bit. Unless you are thinking of ending this visit early?..... You got somewhere else to go ?"

"No bro, it ain't even like that. I know how it is eating prison food. I would have thought that you would be in a rush to eat some street food.

Malachi looked at him as if he was a venerial disease before bursting out laughing.

"Ha,ha. You call the food in the vending machine street food!!??....... You have a lot to learn little brother. There ain't no shrimps or lobster tails in that machine, there ain't no steaks or curry goat or crab legs in that machine."

He let that sink in before continuing,"Besides, I eat street pussy!!!. If you know what I mean. You feel me. So I have access to anything in these machines like I'm the one that stocks these muhfuckas. Your boy ain't losing his swag. Just because I'm locked up, my mind aint locked up. You hear me? I got a bad officer on the roster so I'm Gucci."

K Rouga looked at his older brother and was overcome with fear. He did not know what his brother would say once he told him the reason he had rode all this way to come see him.

Before he had a chance to gather his thoughts, Malachi spoke up once again.

"Tell me something,why are you out here at 8:45 on a Saturday morning? I know people your age usually go to the club on Fridays and sleep until 1 pm on Saturdays. You must really miss me or you in some deep shit. You don't come up here to see me by yourself unless you need money, or you need me to help you put in some wet work!! So tell me which it is ?"

K Rouga mustered up all of the strength that he had in his bones and told himself it was now or never. So he took a deep breath and began,

"You don't hold nothing back as usual so I'm going to just come out and say it bro. I fucked around and shot P Nouchy last night!! It was a matter of respect and I had to do it, or else I would have seemed like a real coward."

Malachi sat up straighter in his chair as he listened to the whole story of the events that led to the actions taken by his younger brother, against his youngest brother.

There was no way to justify the actions undertaken by his brother, however, what could he say? Here he was, locked up for the murder of his best friend for his respect. So it was a situation that was contradictory to even give any input.

Yet it was a situation that was a reality in every hood and in every city, and every state, and every country in the world.

There was no way to fathom the mindset of his brother. This was something that would take all of his intellect to fix. Black lives mattered to Malachi. K Rouga looked in Malachi's eyes and knew that it was more than a thorn in the side of his brother.

K Rouga was high on cocaine and marijuana during the episode with his brother, but he didn't tell Malachi that. It was an unspoken commandment within the family, that if anybody in the family smoked or did any controlled substance there was a price to pay.

K Rouga knew that he did not want to experience the banishment of losing the protection of the family name.

Just the name McClain, Lockhart, and Elmore brought fear to the city and counties in the tri state area. As well as Laurens SC.

It was an honor to be amongst legends in the streets. Past, present, and future. K Rouga knew he was in for a lecture on Family ties, so he just sat back with an open mind to receive the advice that he was desperately in need of.

Malachi began," Let me get this right the first time so it ain't no need to re-establish this shit later...You bought a first-class ticket to South Carolina, from LaGuardia airport in New York City. You traveled all the way down here to tell me that you shot our little brother, over what you refer to as respect??... And you want me to do what for you??!!"

"I want to get you to help me Malachi. I shot him. I know I fucked up. I just had to make a statement. He was treating me like a pussy. I just had to do it."

Malachi raised up to the edge of his seat and snarled at his brother. He took a second to formulate his thoughts before replying.

"You didn't have to do shit little nigga, I don't even use language like this, but you got me super pissed off. First of all, respect is demanded, it is not sought out in the bloodshed of your family. No matter the object of desire, or whatever you think you would have gained by doing so, you come to me expecting me to help you with a problem that is bigger than me.

I'm honestly surprised that you didn't get fucked up in the process. Nouchy has adequate security set up to protect him, so I don't see how you even caught him slipping. You broke a rule in this family yo. I'm not even in any position to extend my opinion to you, because that's something I won't do. I will not choose sides. However, I will tell you that whatever Nouchy decides to do it will be in the best interest of everybody involved, that's the only good thing in your favor other than that I'm through with this conversation ."

"So that's how you gonna do me big bro? " K Rouga exclaimed. " I came all this way for you to help me and you telling me that you can't help me in any way ?"

Malachi took a deep breath before he blew a gasket in his brain. It took him all his restraint to not slap the hell out of his brother. Instead he eased back on his chair and told his brother,

"Is that how I'm gonna do you? Really? First of all you did that to yourself. Whatever you thought you would gain by doing so, is beyond me. But I didn't do anything to you. I'm just telling you that I will not give you anything. What more do you want me to say? "

K Rouga looked at him and begged him," Say that you understand bro.. say that you know what it's like to be in my shoes. Give me some kind of advice on what to do next because I'm begging you... Please big bro!!!"

Malachi dismissed his comments and told him, "I have no advice for you. Now go get me a couple of those chicken sandwiches, and some Skittles,Doritos,two of those pineapple orange sodas, and some of those sour patch candies and make it quick cuz I gotta go catch the NBA playoff game at 12."

K Rouga was shocked that the one person whom he looked up to,would openly and blatantly disregard him in such a way. He got up as he began talking to himself.

"This muhfucka dismissing me like I'm a fucking peon. I got something for his ass."

As soon as he was done getting all of the food Malachi wanted, he dumped it on the table and strode to the exit, not bothering to look back at his brother.

No matter what happened, he would not accept being insulted by anybody. Sometimes blood wasn't thicker than water. It just made the water red!!! K Rouga was now after blood and nobody would stop him from getting it.

The way things were, it was just a matter of time before shit got real but K Rouga was determined to be on point every step of the way. Nobody was going to catch him slippin and he would die for his respect!!!!! If only he knew how true that was.....

Chapter Three

"Let that nigga know that he better show the fuck up tonight. His ass been off the fuckin grid for a couple days, so make sure you remind that nigga that this is a fuckin business not a fuckin hobby. This ain't nothing we do because we want to, it's because we have to." A Rich spoke into his Motorola X touch screen Android phone.

He pulled up his pants as he continued, "This shit is serious L's. We gotta pull 70 cars before this week is up. I spoke to the dealer and he said that there are a few cars on the list that are over the standard. We have some rare cars on it also."

L's ears perked up at the sound of there being rare cars on the list. This meant that they would all be raking in the dough after the mission was over.

"What kind of rare cars are we talking about?" He asked A Rich, as his eyes continued to see money signs.

A Rich laughed to himself because he knew just exactly what his right hand was thinking. He didn't want him to go into a convulsion just thinking about the cars on the list, so he told him what cars they were looking to steal at the next mission.

"The dealer said that there were like...., 3 Maybach Landaulets, 2 Bugatti Veyrons, 1 SSC Ultimate Aera, 1 LeBlanc Mirabeau, a Pagani Zonda Cinque Roadster, 1 Lamborghini Reventon, and 1 Koenigsegg CCXR, a total of at least 10 million worth of super cars, exotic cars at that."

L's felt his mouth begin to water as he said," What kind of take are we looking to pull in after the pie is warmed up and divided?" L's asked A Rich.

A Rich was a light-skinned pretty boy from the blocks of Brooklyn. Most of his family lived in Coney Island, a few blocks away from the boardwalk.

His reach extended well out of the borough of BK, far into the alleys and rat infested corners of all five boroughs.

Standing at 5 foot 5, A Rich was a force to be reckoned with. Being blessed with the right family setting as a child growing up, Andre Richardson had a lot of people he could call in favors from, and all of his companions knew that he could be counted upon to come through in any situation.

His body was tatted up with tattoos of his family, associates,his burough and city, and anything of significance to a person who likes music, guns, women, and drugs. The 4 prong coping method for black men. At least that was what white stereotypical people thought.

He devoted his back piece to the crew that made him a threat. The people that made his life easier. His reign to the middle rung of the ladder was an easy one. And even though he wasn't where he wanted to be in the power 15 amongst Dons and organized leaders, he was well on his way thanks to the Spaceship Money Gang Mafia.

You can almost imagine what the makeup of the "Money Gang Mafia" represented.

Never had the state, counties, and boroughs of New York, seen a pack of more viscous animals, without any discrimination of men, women and children, in any fashion.

If heads had to roll it didn't matter if it was "Apple heads", as kids were known as in the clique. Or if it was "Bobbleheads", as adults were known as.

Any head, meant that it wouldn't be the heads of anyone in the Money Gang Mafia.

Better to kill than to be killed!!!!

This was a motto and a Creed that the Mafia lived by. There was no other way. L's was a prime example of that. Born and raised in Norfolk Virginia, but raised in Cleveland Ohio, L's was captured by the street life. There was nothing more compelling than being able to earn the street credibility that made his name respected and feared by all people of all ages.

From the many sleepless nights sneaking into the living room and filling his drinking cup with his father's brown liquor, to the short school days while skipping class to make a few extra dollars. His path had been clear-cut for him ever since day one when his mother told him, "Lavar honey, I know you are different. I don't expect you to be like anybody else. I love you as you are, because God gave you a smile out of this world!!!", she said as she pinched his cheeks and have him a kiss.Muah!!!

She grabbed him, as he tried to wiggle out of her embrace.

"Stop tickling me mama", he said while shrieking in laughter.

"Boy you know you my tickle me Lavar! Fuck Elmo, you my fuzzy wuzzy Teddy Bop. Come here give Mama some sweet lips" She said as she caught up to him and grabbed him around his neck.

Muah!!! He gave his mother a kiss on the lips. He remembered those days like it was yesterday. How he wished that he could have those days back. He would give anything in his life to have his mother again.

His mother died three years later, the victim of a stray bullet due to gang violence in his neighborhood. Where the fuck was crime watch when a black kid needed their mother fucking ass!!?? Huh!!??

You can't tell me can you!!??.........

Them bitches didn't even stop Trayvon from getting killed!!! So much for the cops wanting to protect and serve.

They did a good job at protecting themselves, and the crooked officers in uniform, and serving up faulty indictments, false subpoenas, false sense of protection, that when it became a situation where Justice would be denied, they would serve us up with a couple hot slugs to protect their self serving interests.

Pure hypocrisy! L's was a victim in more ways than one. When A Rich met up with him by accident in a bad section of Brooklyn, where L's was outnumbered, they had linked up and history was written.

At that time L's was a 6 ft 1, 165 lb, scrawny teenager. His hair only grew in curls. That part of him came from his mother Laura and he never cut his hair after her death.

She was his strength, sort of like Samson. His strength was unimaginable. He made sure to keep his hair maintained as a sacrilege to his mother.

His body was inflicted with scars that he suffered at the hands of the streets. He had tried the group home thing but it wasn't up to his speed so he got the fuck on through.

It was a blessing to meet A Rich. It was a warm summer night and the street lights had just been turned on. A Rich was sitting on the steps to his project building. Just chilling, nothing to do tonight... he thought to himself.

His on/off again girlfriend was at a baby shower, and he really didn't chill with dudes his age because as you know, a crowd of black people would create an environment of discomfort for the citizens who were afraid of the crowd so they would call the cops.

And the crowd of black boys were afraid of the cops when they came. Ever since George Floyd had been killed at the hands of the police, there was little trust with the police and for the police.

The days had come and gone where citizens called the police for help.

They would rather go and purchase a gun, pepper spray,stun guns, and whatever else they felt they needed to protect themselves, than to call the cops and risk being killed or hurt by an untrained police officer, or a police officer who had no level of understanding whatsoever.

A Rich was posted in front of the 4 building on 27th Street and Surf avenue, when he saw a multitude of people flying past him in pursuit of a light-skin dude, who was kicking up rocks and using the sidewalk as a treadmill.

"What the fuck is going on ?" A Rich thought to himself, as he raced down the block in pursuit of all the action.

Shiddd, this was better than sitting on the damn steps and waiting on his chick to call him.

"Let's get it", he said to himself.

As he approached the scene he saw that the crowd has surrounded the young dude and was talking shit to him, as they had him in a human ping pong match, tossing and shoving him into each other.

"Why the fuck you down on our strip motherfucker?", said the first dude who reminded A Rich of a short Bo Jackson.

He was real stocky and he looked like he would do damage.

"This nigga ain't the dude we looking for cuz", said the second goon in the squad, who reminded A Rich of a light-skinned Tyrese Gibson.

Pretty ass nigga with no fight game.

"Fuck that!! This nigga is a bitch who lives on Neptune! We ain't having that trash over here on Surf. Fuck that shit let's beat his ass!!!"

A Rich said to himself, "Hold up don't none of these niggas live on Surf!!"

A Rich began to get angry with what he was seeing because he had always been taught to stand up to anyone trying to be a bully. To him or anyone else.

He began to walk towards the commotion and screamed out," Hold the fuck up, Don't none of y'all niggas live on Surf. Y'all come down here perpetrating and shit, trying to beat on this man. Y'all niggas live on Mermaid. So all of y'all need to get the fuck out of my hood with the bullshit!!"

"Who the fuck do you think you talking to cuz?", said the dude who looked like Bo Jackson.

"Ain't no cuz shit around here homeboy. It's only Big B's over here, so if you ain't trying to get your blood pumped out your body, get the fuck off my set."

"BLATTTT!!!BLATTTT!! SUWOOOOOP!!! SUWOOOOOP!!!"

A Rich let off a call to alert the homies in the building to the traitors who were in his neighborhood.

Seeing that the situation was about to get from worse to grave, common sense told the culprits to get the hell out of there and be on point.

The one who was acting like the ringleader didn't want to allow the victim to get off without a scratch, yet it just wasn't worth it right now.

"I'm going get you lil nigga. Matter fact, I'ma get both of y'all." He said as he began to move backwards.

A Rich began to feel his anger getting the best of him as he kept walking towards the culprits,

"Both of y'all better get to steppin like Chris Brown in stomp the Yard, before you lose your life lil nigga. We ain't about to keep jaw jackin back and forth, make a move, or shut the fuck up. Matter fact, come over here Red",he said as he pointed at the little dude they had surrounded.

As L's started to move past everyone, the block became infested with red bandanas and all you heard was weapons being cocked and loaded.

"Yo cuz, let's break out these niggas ain't worth the trouble", said the second goon. Anyone who was out there could look into his eyes and see that he didn't want any kind of trouble or any kind of action.

A Rich spoke up again and told him,"Listen to your ppls and break loose homeboy, before it be a lot of mommas ordering black dresses. I know your mama wouldn't mind, but think for your comrades. Coming down here automatically deserves war. We don't fuk with none of y'all niggas on Mermaid or Neptune. So brace yourself and make like a slim fat yogurt and get light". He said to the one who was obviously in charge.

A Rich didn't hesitate to speak his mind on any level which was why he had love in the hood but sometimes being vocal came with a lot of drama outside of the comforts of Surf Ave.

But even then, he was ready for whatever.

The leader of the pack defiantly stood still before A Rich and looked in his eyes as he etched his face into his mind.

He wanted to burn his image into his mind, of a person that he was going to hunt down and unmercifully slaughter!!

Nobody had ever talked to him with such blatant disrespect and had stayed alive to talk about it. After a minute or two, he had had enough of the moment and silently motioned to his crew to move out.

They left the block short of accomplishing their goal of beating up an innocent person, but had gained a new territory beef that looked like it would be detrimental to alot of people's lives before it was over with.

That's the price that you had to pay sometimes in order to make it in the world. Live or die by the decisions you make.

After the departure of the outsiders, A Rich was left to explain why he had done what he had done. Many wanted to know why he had intervened for a nigga who didn't even live on Surf.

Alot of homies felt that it was a waste of time to step in on behalf of another nigga who would have gotten his just due. After all, that was how it went down in gang wars .

A Rich didn't feel the need to explain, but for the sake of those who looked up to him he told the crowd of homies that stayed behind after the excitement was over,

"First of all, this is our Hood!!! WE run this whole strip from 25th to 28th Street. That's SURF! Our territory!. So what we do on our block, ain't no way in the hell I'm going to let another nigga do without our permission. If a nigga can't come to our hood and sell a dime bag of weed or a vial of crack, he can't come to our hood to get his steam off on anybody."

He paused before continuing, "Whether or not this nigga is from Surf aint why I stopped it from happening. But if we are we allowing niggas to come up in our house, and just do what the fuck they want to, then it becomes a open invitation, a fuckin house party. And to be honest with you, personally, I'm not with that type of shit because sooner or later somebody gonna feel some type of way, and we gonna have to smash them the fuck out."

A Rich began to look around and saw that he had their full attention and most of them were nodding their heads in affirmation. So he decided to continue giving them jewels of wisdom.

"Then, not only does that bring unnecessary heat to the hood, but that brings more bad than good. I'm comfortable in my hood without having the police coming over here, trying to shine flashlights in my face and look up my ass, trying to see if I'm stashing crack in my asscrack. Y'all niggas gotta see shit for what it really is.

Every move I make,I make it for the hood to shine. Because when I shine, you shine, we shine, G Shine. All Day!!!"

Without waiting to hear what they had to say in return, he grabbed the light-skin dude and motioned him towards his building. And from that day on, L's was indebted to A Rich for saving his ass and standing up to his own set in the process.

(BACK TO PRESENT DAY)

"I'm going to make sure that forgetful ass negro shows his ass up bro. I know we got a lot riding on it. If it's one thing I've learned from you, is to be punctual and on time. I'm about to get at bro and holla back at you before 5. I know the others should be on point. Say ?....Did you make sure the lotto numbers matched up?"

L's was referring to the authorization code that was on the master vaults at the Federal Bureau impound lot. Alot of people didn't know what happened to the thousands of cars that the feds confiscated annually.

It was well known within the Bureau that whatever cars were seized could be kept by the seizing officer, only if the suspect was murdered or dead on arrival.

That way, it wouldn't produce a paper trail. To be dishonest was to be certain that it didn't lead back to you.

The other alternative was that the feds kept cars that were seized at the federal impound lot for safekeeping, until they could be auctioned off at the designated spots designed for acquiring the most funds that the cars would attract. In other words, more bang for the buck!!!

There wasn't much that money couldn't buy you. With the incentive for creating a steady income for her family, federal agent Tamika Richardson, who was also A Richs distant cousin, supplied the Spaceship Money Gang with addresses and other vital information on locations of FBI warehouses.

These warehouses housed the cars after they were transported to the FBI impound lot. The reason for doing so was because after the cars had been transported, it would take months to years depending on the outcome of a civil trial,or legal trial, to determine if the cars would remain seized, or if the cars would be returned to the owner.

If they were to remain seized, they would be taken to warehouses and loaded to the trucks that would be used to transport them to the auction sites.

That information for the vehicles would be erased from the federal database and given it to the owner of the auction site who would handle the transaction and load money into offshore accounts of agents, local businessman,senators, congressmen, and the likes.

Once in the hands of the SMM (Spaceship Money Gang Mafia), the cars were distributed to a few different venues in mostly western states, such as California, Detroit, Arizona. And a few eastern states, such as New York, New Jersey, Connecticut.

Even though A Rich didn't want to deal cars in the tri-state area, he had not yet branched out his operation to be overseen by other individuals in different areas.

Simply because everything that he gave of himself to be successful in pursuit of money, respect, happiness, prosperity, he tended to hold close to his chest, close to his heart.

He was not yet prepared to allow anybody, any part of that, and then have his dreams come crashing down because their sentimental value,or their emotional attachment, wasn't aligned with his.

So for A Rich he was content with the tri-state area for now, but he knew that he had to expand his operation elsewhere in order to be safe in the future.

Loose lips, sunk ships, and there was no way in hell that he was going to allow his life to be reduced to a cell that was smaller than a walk in closet.

After all, it was a very lucrative business to be involved in. Yet, A Rich also knew how it was to become so caught up in the process of everything, and the financial windfall, that one would become flashy, flamboyant, arrogant, which was why he forced himself to lead a boring lifestyle aside from the lifestyle of the Rich and famous.

Because that way it kept him grounded and with the awareness that all of this could be taken away from him and he would be back at square one.

Not to mention the fact that he would have people who unknowingly helped him out if the Feds ever came to question them about him.

Knowing that by him giving the impression of a hood niggga,who had a hood girlfriend,drove a hooptie, and banged the color red with the rest of the hood, that's what the hell they would relate to the feds.

The feds were known in the hood as, Forever Involved in Bullshit, or Forever Bullying Innocent people.

He knew what he had to do and he did it well. He also doubted that L's would be inclined to ever snitch him out in any way shape or form.That was out of the question.

"You already know that these codes is official like a sponsor for the NBA! Have I ever come half steppin when it came to this business??. I know it's only been like 7 months of doing this operation, but trust in me like the Jews trust in Jesus. I got you.

I'm not a newborn into this world... Shiddddd by the way, the split is 10% of every car we sell, and 45% of of every car we have to chop up. Some of the cars have no VIN number so it's a no go to go the dealership. We expect to get enough cars to send some to the dealership though. I'm still looking to open the dealership in Tampa. I spoke to Juice Bagger and he made the down payment on the lot.

We will be able to finance the first and second shipment of cars from overseas, leaving us with a safety net to fall back on in case of the worst that could happen. You just better make sure we have all of our drivers tonight!!!" A rich told L's.

L's pulled on the blunt he was smoking and allowed the smoke to fill his lungs before replying to A Rich,

"I love that ratio, you know I'm going to handle my end. I'll make the calls now and I'll get at you around 5 sometime."

" Spaceship", replied Arich.

" Money Gang" he responded.

" No I's,"

" Just Us."

A Rich hung up the phone and was getting ready to finish getting dressed, when the blonde that he had entertained the night before grabbed him by the belt buckle and pulled him close.

"Come here big daddy ",she murmured in an alluring voice.

"What you want lil ma ?",he asked her. Already knowing that she wanted more of that loving that he put on her. Shit was real and he knew she wanted another sample of the Vanilla Ice Cream that he had by the cases!

"Give me my blowpop so I can suck that muhfucka like you like it boo..." She said as she began to lick her lips and twirl her tongue between her lips.

"Girl if you want this dick you gotta go for what you know. I'm not into giving myself to just anybody," he said with a hint of sarcasm and a smirk on his face.

"Boy, get your sexy ass over here ", Tiffany said as she undid the belt buckle on his pants as he sat back on the bed and let her do the do with his "females favorite" blowpop.

He thought to himself, "I can get used to this shit." He knew that most women couldn't get enough of the way he held the dick on them. He had eight inches of what he referred to as "Geronimo Pratt", for all of those who was willing to be tamed.

As he laid back and enjoyed getting a blowjob of his life, his phone began to vibrate and play the automatic ringtone that he had been waiting to hear for a few days.

"Stay scheming..... Niggas tryna get at me.... I'll ride for my nigga dogggggggg.... I'll slide for my nigga...."

The song was playing on repeat customary with how ringtones were.

It was enough to make Tiffany stop what she was doing and say," Are you going to get that, or you want me to suck ya dick to the beat?"

He laughed at her and told her, "Do what you do, how you do it,and why you do it, and let me handle this!"

Before she could respond with a smartass comment, he shoved his hard dick in her mouth and said, "Take that Dick".

He swiped the phone icon and said "Yoooooo what's good fool?"

"Whats good big homie?" K Rouga responded.

" Fuck you got going on negro,you've been off the grid for way too long. Seems like you've been in a hornet's nest. We couldn't find you anywhere my dude."

A Rich smiled to himself because when he knew he was lying to K Rouga. He knew the whereabouts of every one of his people just like he knew that L's was fucking around with one of his baby mamas.

A problem not big enough to demand attention at the moment, but a problem that needed fixing before it became a cancer. There would be time for that.

K Rouga cleared his throat before speaking," I've been dealing with family issues which is why I called you fam. I need your outreach and your expertise in a few matters dealing with my peeps. I really can't do what I want, or need to do, without your sources. I may need a couple of your contacts at the network."

"The Network", was an elite group of hired assassins known for handling any and everything that was thrown their way. Nobody was exempt from the clutches and grasps of the network.

Very few could get into the immediate circle of the network because it was family owned and operated. But somehow A Rich was able to earn the trust of one of his cellmates cousins at Attica, and that in turn led to an alliance for the ages.

However, the family didn't sell or deal in the processing or distribution of drugs. The only thing that they did was, partake in the distribution of body parts. That was what made them productive in everything that they acquired.

The network was strictly run by the underground cartel ran by the infamous Belliano Mobster Family. Known for their signature neckties when someone's tongue was pulled through a hole in their neck.

The Belliano Mobster Family, were the ones to contact to handle these issues.

"Slow downnnnnnn.." A Rich began as he grabbed Tiffany's head and brought it back and forth, controlling the tempo of how fast he wanted her to suck his dick.

After getting the tempo right without his hands, he continued," Put that track on pause for a second baby bro. First things first. You know when you want something, you always call me, but when you need to show your ass up to work for me you always slacking. That shit ends today. No threat, strictly truth. Am I clear ?"

K Rouga was taken aback for a second and stammered on his words before he replied," Yes you are clear bro." He stated with more enthusiasm than needed but A Rich let it slide as he stated, "Okay now that we have that established, let me remind you that we have a show tonight. I hope you haven't forgotten that you are the lead actor".

Meaning that K Rouga was one of the drivers for the car heist. A Rich wanted to emphasize how serious he was about tonight so he continued" You really gonna make me murk yo ass if you don't show up."

Even though A Rich said it with a laugh, it was deliberate enough to let Kendrick know that this was where the bucking tendencies stopped. It wouldn't be tolerated anymore. No matter who it was, anybody was dispensable or expendable.

"I'ma be there, you don't have to threaten me with that New York shit son... I'm going to be onstage at the right moment to do this show and I'm going to be onstage to receive my awards. Just let me know if you can come through for me.

A Rich was so caught up in what Tiffany was doing to his balls, that for a second he began to moan into the phone.. Then remembering that he was still on a call he replied to K Rouga,

"You know you wouldn't have even come to me if you thought I couldn't handle whatever you needed me to do. Why don't you give me an outline of what you need".

"Okay it's like this............"

As A Rich listened to what was being asked of him, Tiffany continued to suck away like she was the last woman on earth and A Rich was the last man.

A Rich listened to the thoughts of revenge by a brother scorned.

Such a shame how loyalty was replaced by greed,lust for money, power and respect. It was a shame that the price of a soul could be bought anywhere from a piece of crack, or a big eight, or a double up, to next to nothing but reparations based on bad principles and doctrines based off of selfishness.

Life had begun to take on a new meaning, because of how people saw life as a mere token of admission into elite circles, similar to" The Network". It may not have been as elaborate as The Network, but it was there. It was circles of greed and even in the circle to fight for power was evident.

It wasn't up to A Rich to be the "grim reaper", but he was known as The harvest in "The Network". He planted the seeds and the others killed the weeds, so that the finances could grow to proportions that everyone could live with.

Everyone loved to live lavish and not have to worry about poverty ever again. Well, at least the ones who were alive.

After listening to the sickness of the whole logic behind the whole deal and what was proposed by K Rouga, A Rich informed him that if everything went ok tonight he would have a deal.

"Say no more. Good looks on this big homie." K Rouga replied.

"Anything worth living for..." A Rich began....

"Is worth dying for!" K Rouga finished off..

"Flesh of my flesh....."

"Blood of my blood."

"Zip.. Trey..Ace!!"

"B 2 Da L."

After hanging up with Rouga, A Rich called L's and told him what happened. L's asked him, "You really fuckin wit this one ? "

A Rich Replied,"Might as well. We both know that killing Nouchy would put us up a level higher on the ladder. I don't mind escorting him to "Ground Hog City", in order for a spot in the limelight.."

"True that.. I'll make that call to Belliano and set some shit up.. We'll link up after the show.. Til then it's Murkin Season.."

A Rich hung up and focused on giving Tiffany some more of his Vanilla icing.. He had alot to do and so little time to do it. It was now or never!!!!!

Chapter Four

"Allahu Akbar".

"Allahu Akbar".

"Al hamdu lillahi rabbil al-amin".

Nouchy was secluded in the lower room of the mosque in the central part of Hoboken, New Jersey. He had called ahead and gained entrance through the bottom chamber, from his mentor and confidante Imam Jafar.

He had known about Islam since his "unofficial" brother Malachi introduced it to him on visit one Friday evening, while he was on visit at the correctional facility.

He had yet to take his "Shahadah" or his (Declaration of Faith), but he felt as if the religion of Islam had a part to play in his life.

Malachi had introduced him to a fellow Muslim brother in the state of South Carolina. Imam Tamir. Who in turn, introduced Nouchy to Imam Jafar.

Imam Jafar was heavily regarded as someone who people loved to be around and whom people admired because he was 100% Authentic and genuine.

For everything that he said, he had a verse in the Quran to back it up. Sometimes he didn't quote the verses,but when he was really in his "mode", he was very much able to do so.

Nouchy was heavily sedated on Ibuprofen 3's,extra strength. He didn't want to take a higher dosage because that would most likely make him groggy and disoriented.

He would have been sedated on liquor too, but he did not want to defoul the sanctified place of worship to many.

DISRESPECT was not to be permitted at any cost while inside this place of worship. That would be like intentionally causing harm to someone's way of life. It would be taken as an insult and it would not be taken lightly.

As Imam Jafar entered into the room he spoke in Arabic,

"Assalam alaikum my brother",(peace be upon you) . He was dressed in a long garment that looked similar to a dress that covered his whole body,yet,left his feet uncovered.

Nouchy often wondered what he would look like if he chose to wear those kind of clothes. Now that he thought about it, he would have to see about getting a couple Muslim outfits. It might bring him alot of positive energy from the atmosphere.

"Walaikum assalam Rahmahtuallah" (Peace and blessings be upon you) Nouchy replied, in the customary greeting that he had heard so many times before.

He had learned a few things from his brother that had helped him grow on so many levels.It had turned him into a person who was not the typical "Hothead" that you saw on a daily basis in the streets. One with no sense of direction or purpose. Or someone who didn't have any kind of guidance. Whatsoever.

These lessons that Nouchy learned, contributed to making him humble and thankful, as well as very knowledgeable in various areas, and it gave him a chance to be open-minded and to be able to be diverse and have relationships with many people outside of the normal crowd, that someone his age would be expected to hang out with.

Which in turn gave him more places to go, when he needed to get away from the city life of New York. He always loved it when he could "dip out" and go somewhere that nobody could find him at.

It was similar to looking for a needle in a haystack.

Imam Jafar pulled out a prayer rug, from the stack of prayer rugs that was neatly folded in a linen closet located near the back door where Nouchy had just come in from. After placing it on the floor and making sure it was smooth, he motioned to Nouchy to join him as he sat down on the prayer rug and crossed his legs.

After Nouchy made his way over to the Imam and sat down, Imam Jafar spoke to him in a low tone.

"What brings you to my place of business ? You do know that worship is a 9 to 5 in itself, and it happens to be the only job in the world that will benefit you in the end. If you so choose to pledge Your Life to God!".

The Imam studied the young man in front of him and could visibly see that something was wrong. This wasn't the usual cheerful visit that they were accustomed to having. He did not want to rush into the conversation so he paused for a minute before continuing,

"Seeing as though you have come across some unpleasantries of your own, you seem to need it all the more. Don't you think ?" He asked Nouchy.

Nouchy could feel every bone in his leg throbbing with pain and regretted that he wasn't a little bit higher off the ibuprofen capsules that he had taken. "If only I had gotten some more out the car before I came in", he thought to himself.

Brought out of his thoughts by the sounds from within the mosque of little children playing upstairs, and unfamiliar chants in Arabic coming from someone who was either reciting the Quran, or they was having a bad day singing, Nouchy looked into Imam Jafar's eyes and responded,

" Yes I need it. In the worse way. It seems as though I am going through the most at the same time and I am starting to become overwhelmed." He said as he tried balancing his foot on top of the crutch that his homegirl had borrowed from the hospital she worked at.

Imam Jafar responded, "Worship is a good way to get your mind away from the hustle and bustle of everyday life. It gives you a chance to come back to the rememberance of your Creator. Besides, it's always a pleasure to see you my dear friend."

Nouchy smiled because the Imam never forced the conversations, because he knew that Nouchy would eventually get to the reason he was there. He was a good listener, and a master of patience.

The only place he was in a rush to go to, was, Paradise and only God had those reservations on lock, so he had to take it easy like the Easy Comfort sneakers he wore on his feet.

Nouchy began, "Ahk,(Brother) I'm in a bind, and I know I must make a decision. A decision that will save my face in the streets. And one that I will not regret. Because as I previously told you, you know that my mother is on her deathbed..."

Imam Jafar listened attentively with the attention span of a student, learning from a scholar, while Nouchy relayed to him what had transpired since the last time they had been in touch.

When Nouchy was done, he asked him," What do you want to do to your brother?" He could have asked the question and continued to probe deeper for the reasons behind what he had heard, but he felt as if that wasn't important at this moment of time.

Imam Jafar understood that Nouchy was here to come to terms and to make Peace with whatever decision he had already made mentally. Otherwise he would not have even taken the time to come to visit him. So he gave

Nouchy his space to fill him in on what he wanted him to know. Thus, he would not press him for too much information.

" I honestly want to hurt him back", Nouchy replied with hurt in his eyes.

Jafar could tell that this was true, but he knew and sensed that Nouchy didn't really want to hurt his brother so he decided to give him jewels of wisdom.

"Does the streets mean more to you than your family ties? Does your brother's life and blood hold more value to you, than the streets? Does life hold no significant value for your family, or the family that you will leave behind should anything happen to you?"

He allowed a few seconds of silence to follow his words before he continued,

"These are all questions that you have to answer truthfully within yourself. I sense your dilemma my son. And I hope that you know I will never tell you to shed the blood of a relative. That would be against the life that I lead. It is against Islam to kill. Within certain boundaries."

Seeing that Nouchy was wrestling with something in his mind, Imam Jafar continued,

"However, it is permissible to do what has been done to you, to the other person. Transgression or should I say, retaliation for being transgressed against, cannot be more than what has happened to you. Let me explain, since this is why we live by the term an eye for an eye.

If you were to harm me and pluck out my eye, I could not do anything more to you than to pluck your eye out as recompense for my eye. Not that I can see out of these dusty spectacles anyway... Ha ha ha.. but you get my analogy." He said as he sat still to see if Nouchy would respond.

Oftentimes, Nouchy knew that the wisdom and insight from Imam Jafar was far from over so he just remain seated and waited for more wisdom. Over the years Imam Jafar had become a source for strength and refuge, and Nouchy trusted and loved him as he loved his own father.

After a while of the stalemate silence, Imam Jafar continued on. "While I just gave you that advice, on another note, I would be remiss to tell you that you must not seek retribution for the satisfaction of someone else. These "streets" as you seldomly refer to, the filth and garbage out there in society, have no true concern for you or your people. The concrete jungle only wants more blood to line the cracks in the sidewalk with it.

As if our blood has not been shed enough!. It is a permanent fixture on the roads all across America. Across the whole world for that matter. The bullet only want names on them so they can find a way to hit their target. And they don't discriminate. The death Angel has a job to do everyday, without any of us making it any more easier for him. It saddens me that you would possibly want to stoop to the level of your brother, but you must do what you decide to do for you."

Imam Jafar took a second to ponder his words before continuing,

"Only you can make a decision. This decision must be solely for you. Like I said, there are innocent people to be brought into this violence by your deliberate actions, so you must think of those who don't want to get involved in this situation. Those are the ones who will lose out the most.

Nowadays people believe that violence can solve everything, yet it can only do what it was intended to do. And that is cause and bring destruction to any and everything that it touches. Nothing good can come to the person who is befallen with the wrath of God.!!

Do you want the blood of your brother to be on your hands? Your blood has already been sacrificed to the Earth as recreational nutrients for the ground and dirt. So you must be cautious and knowingly make a choice that will not be detrimental to you or anyone else. Do you get where I'm coming from? How do you feel?".

Nouchy thought for a minute before he spoke. He had been taught to listen,to analyze, assess, and then speak. He had his mind made up already, but the Imam had unknowingly reassured him in his decision.

He began," To be honest, I don't want no problems. At least not with my own family. I don't see the use of bringing harm to my own brother. Regardless of what happened. I'm willing to forgive him of his trespasses against me. Yet, I know what kind of backlash that the streets will have for me right now."

Imam Jafar started to speak but saw that Nouchy was not finished so he stayed silent.

Nouchy continued," I will bite the bullet again, for the sake of bringing peace to the situation. I cannot say that I am an advocate for peace and go out in the streets and act a damn fool. On the contrary, I do want my just due, in exercising the right to shoot his ass a couple of times. Excuse my poor manners for cursing in the mosque. To be honest, I know the ties of kinship and I truly want for my brother what I want for myself.

I want him to have life! What do I look like, if I personally escort my brother to the Angel of death? So I am going to swallow my pride on this one. But I'm going to tell you, that I won't be so forgiving next time. And just so you know, I will need extra sessions in the gym as soon as my legs get better. Give me two weeks. I have some aggression I need to get off my chest. Haha.

Imam Jafar looked at him and smiled. He reminded him so much of himself when he was younger. The way he thought, and the way he carried himself. It was very uncanny when he thought about it.

He took a minute to gather his thoughts before he spoke. This gave him time to think about what had been said to him and to give the appropriate response.

"My son, first of all, you must not think about the backlash that the streets will have for you. Because at the end of the day, the streets will not be the one to take you out of this situation. The streets will not be anything but a force of evil in pressuring and persuading you to do the opposite of what you intend to do. You must heal spiritually, and release the flow of evil from within the recesses of your mind.

Only then will you heal physically. That way you will be in tune with your soul, and consciousness, at the same time. You need to focus and become one with yourself and get yourself together for the journey to come. The only thing that can come out of the situation is what you desire. Yet, you must also be aware that by you choosing not to retaliate, you open yourself to the criticism of others.

It takes a strong mind not to be dictated by the actions or words of others. You possess the unteachable ability to let things roll off of your shoulders. So you will get past the chaos. However the world is full of revolving doors, so you must be willing to stand in the face of adversity, and you can't waiver.

Not even when the streets tell you that it smells blood. You have to be a stone in the foundation that you wish to stand upon. You cannot be weak and expect your foundation to stand intact. It will never work. You have to stand guard against the evil thoughts, that will plague you. The thoughts telling you that you have made the wrong decision.

You must battle your own mind and remain convinced that you did the right thing for yourself and others. The only one you have to answer to is Allah(God). Make your bed with comfortable thoughts so you can rest assured at night. Anything else doesn't matter."

He looked at Nouchy and felt in his heart that things would be alright.

Imam Jafar felt at peace with the outcome of this situation. Albeit might be a temporary outcome. It was still one that he could be proud of. Seeing that this issue was resolved for the moment he decided to change the mood.

"Now that we have that settled, we have another matter to settle on this chess board. You know nobody challenges me like you do?"

Nouchy was glad that he had come to his mentor for advice. He was happy with the outcome and now it was time to kick some ass on the chessboard.

"Come on then Sensai, I will oblige you and your daily fix of supplements. Because you lose every time you take me on. I have a few new tricks up my sleeve that I want to try on you." He told Imam Jafar.

"I would say the same thing but I have no sleeves on my garment...Ha ha ha.." Imam Jafar replied, in an attempt to lighten up the mood.

"You first elder",

"Much obliged starlight".

Nouchy fought to focus while playing chess, as he prayed that he was making the best decision of his life. He hoped he would not regret it but somehow he knew he would.

Imam Jafar knew the look of despair on his young proteges face. He himself, was once a "street thug". One who had taken the streets hostage before he came into the folds of Islam.

He also knew that if push came to shove, and the gloves were pulled off, he would be right there to swing and fight by the side of the Young Lion in his presence.

He began to pray, " Let not the burden of my brother be too much. Let not the pain of his soul cause civil unrest and thus cause the tide of trouble to submerge him. Let not the Fate be upon him to be caught in harm's way. I pray for myself as well that I have gotten him to the path of righteousness. I pray that his soul be light in the darkness. Please watch over those of us who are servants of peace, and let it not be the blood of the transgressors that drown the light that you have ignited within. La Iliha Ill Allah(There is no God but Allah).

Even after the prayer Imam Jafar felt an uneasiness about the situation and advised Nouchy to stay in Hoboken until he healed.

Nouchy looked at him and said," I will be around. I don't want to burden you Imam."

Imam Jafar scoffed at his comment and replied" Nonsense. I will always be around for you to beat up on in chess. Always know that my love for you runs deep. Your battles are mines also. Just don't make me come out of retirement. I still have my old pair of Jordans still in the closet and my Evisu sweatsuit. My monkey suit. I'll go ape shit if and when I need to."

He laughed as he continued," Those were the days I'm going to go to hell for. But it was worth it. Just know that I'm here for you. I got your back kid. know that ... !!"

Nouchy was overcome with emotions because he knew these words to be true. He felt safe in knowing that he had a true friend and a comrade that had his best interests at heart and was very grateful to have met him when he did.

In the back of both of their minds simultaneously they both thought... If this hits the fan, we will need Him!!

Chapter Five

"Where the stash at pussy?"

JuiceBagger had the barrel of a Glock 17 pointed to his head, as he was led to his brand new red and black Mazda 3i sport sedan.

He did not know how he had ended up in this position in the first place. Or how they had gotten up on him so fast without his "6th Sense" kicking in.

A couple seconds ago he was in a restaurant, closing a deal and feeling nothing but optimism for the future, to now being held at gunpoint and being wary of the future. Talk about a drastic shift of events!!!

Here he was with a couple of an unidentifiable people with masks on, escorting him to his car after a meeting with his clients in a Sizzler's restaurant in White plains New York.

"What stash are y'all talkin about ? I don't sell drugs if that's what y'all after. I sell art. I'm an artist. I paint pictures.....

SMACK!!!

Giovanni smacked him across the head with the barrel of the Glock 17, as he told him, "Shut the fuck up you fuckin nerd. We ain't ask you what you do. We know what the fuck you do. You are a Black Picasso in the making. We've seen some of your work lil nigga. We aren't worried about you. We know that you're tied in with them Chain Gang Empire niggas so don't even fuckin play games."

JuiceBagger instantly grew apprehensive of what was about to go down. Simply because these idiots knew who he was, and who he was in alliance with, and he knew nothing about them at all. This would be a tricky situation that he had to be very careful as to what he did, and said. Because the wrong move could possibly cost him more than he was willing to pay. His life.

"We ain't come here to play with your punk ass. We are only going to ask you one more time. And if your answer doesn't satisfy our needs, we will satisfy the needs of Smith & Wesson." Giovanni told him as his fingers gripped the barrel of the gun tighter.

JuiceBagger looked around for some glimmer of hope. Hoping that a passerby would come to his aid. Or that one of his clients had forgotten to tell him something, and would be coming to speak to him, and stumble upon the scene. All he needed was to buy himself a little time in order to sort things out.

He wasn't in a position to be disloyal to the crew that had emerged as his family. In his line of work, discretion was the key to survival. There was no tolerance for any form of insubordination, or any sign of weakness. Weakness was to include being vulnerable to the temptations, that led to the downfall of so many individuals who strived for power in the history of mankind.

There could be no room for any mistake when it came to the security of the Empire. The Empire was founded by a circle of friends that was locked up with JuiceBagger when he was incarcerated in the state of South Carolina.

It had started off as a minor rap group, but with all relationships and bonds in human nature, things evolved in the group and the group evolved into more than just rappers.

JuiceBagger decided to give up the 50 thousand that he had in his glove compartment box. It would make him lose out on 50 thousand in cash, but that was a small price to pay. Because after all, if you were dead, you couldn't make any money.

Even though it was a blow to his pride, it was nothing that he could do about it at the present moment in time. So it was better for him to do what these hooligans wanted him to do, even though his pride would take the brunt of it.

"You know what?", JuiceBagger began as he continued to control his breathing. He didn't want anyone to get excited and make a false move. His life depended on it and he was looking to diffuse the situation as expeditiously as possible.

"You guys can have the money, the car,my watch my clothes,whatever makes y'all happy. Just take whatever y'all came for. The money is in the glove compartment. It's 50 Grand. It's a grand in my jeans pockets, and here are the keys to the car. Please just take it and go. " He reached in his pocket for the keys, that he kept next to the switchblade that he had stashed in the pocket of his jeans in case of emergencies.

This situation definitely qualified as an emergency. The knife was a 8 Inch Tak Force Assisted Open, Pearl Handle Folding Pocket Knife. It even came with his name engraved on it in gold with the handle displaying the word "Juice" on it. It was made from Japanese surgical steel.

The first time that JuiceBagger saw it, he had to admit that it looked real good!! Real beautiful. But he doubted that it would feel good if it was used on him.

Just as his hand closed over the blade, he was compensated for his efforts with another slap to the face, and a crack across the head with the pistol.

SMACK!!!! PLOP!!!!

" AHGHHRRHGHRGH!!!! What the fuck!!!!",he cursed as he began to grab at his eye that felt as if it was hanging out of the socket. He knew he had to deescalate the situation, even though he felt he had done nothing wrong to escalate it to the point of him being struck with the gun.

"What's the problem??? I'm giving you what you want", He said as he felt a massive headache coming on. He also couldn't see out of his left eye. These hooligans hadn't come to the arena to play fair.

Giovanni couldn't believe the fact that this dude had over fifty grand on him!!! All they had known was that he was a part of the small group of dope boys who sold drugs in the hood.

The encounter was a chance encounter, which happened as Giovanni and his right-hand man Hazel, had taking his mother to Sizzlers to celebrate her 60th birthday.

It was a once in a lifetime milestone in the making. So they had both chipped in from months of selling weed, and stealing clothes and selling them. It had cost them a grip to make sure her 60th birthday was one worth remembering but you only lived once and that was all that mattered to them.

Giovanni grabbed JuiceBagger and began to pistol-whip him unmercifully. He wasn't going him because he had done anything. He just wanted to make sure that JuiceBagger forgot this encounter.

Yet he began to get so enraged, because of how his life had turned out, that he had forgotten what he was doing until Hazel grabbed him and slapped the shit out of him.

SLAPPPPP!!!!!

"What the fuck you think you doing stupid ass?!! You better calm the fuck down before you kill this nigga. We only came for the money. Money that he can't report to the police. We didn't get a second damn chance in life, to blow it by killing his mother fuckin ass. We still got my damn mama up in the restaurant, waiting on us to finish our "smoke break", so you need to bring it down a notch and focus on what the fuck we came to do."

Hazel began to look around and check the scene before continuing,

"Check the nigga pockets and get them keys from him. So we can be out. Even if this nigga don't have 50 bands in the glove box, this muhfuckin car will be enough for us. And take that watch off his arm, and that diamond bracelet and let's go.!!"

Giovanni look at the crumpled up form of JuiceBagger and felt no type of remorse. It was either him or another nigga. That's how the streets were. Here today, gone tomorrow. On top of the world today. On the bottom of the world the next!

He looked down at his clothes and knew that he had to make a clean getaway.

"I can't go back in there like this Hazel, I have blood all over my clothes. So you will have to go back in there dolo(alone), and just take your mom's home after y'all eat. I'm just going to go ahead and take this car and everything else to the spot,and I guess we can meet later on tonight around 1 a.m. I'll be up. I gotta swing by and holla at Kombat anyway."

Hazel didn't really trust Giovanni, now that he was going to have all of the "loot" and the Mazda 3i. But he wasn't about to make a scene when he knew where Giovanni stayed and he knew he would find him if he played the game fucked up.

But instead of going with his intuition, which was telling him not to go forward with letting Giovanni out of his sight, Hazel looked at him and said, "Okay bro do what you do. Just don't fuck nothing else up."

Giovanni began to laugh in an attempt to lighten up the mood." I got you bro. He told Hazel, as he paused to look as JuiceBagger before he continued, "I'm about to slide. Go holla at your mom's and just tell her that I had to go and do something for my baby moms. Make up a lie. Hell, you know thats your fucking specialty. Nigga you be lying like a motherfuking Persian rug.... Hahaha".

Hazel laughed at him and told him," It ain't my fault that you don't care about hurting a muhfuckas feelings with the truth. You got ice in your veins, but I fuck wit you bro. I'ma swerve on you later on in the day. Lemme go kick it wit my moms and enjoy the rest of the night with her. Drive careful and don't get a ticket in the new whip. You know how you love to drive super fast nigga".

Giovanni dapped him up and then proceeded to search JuiceBagger and relieve him for everything that he had on his body as JuiceBagger began moaning.

Giovanni laughed to himself as he gathered up all the items and stumbled across the switchblade in JuiceBaggers hand. Instantly he turn into another kind of monster and all of his sudden his childhood demons come loose.

He proceeded to violently stabbed him in his back as he became possessed like a man who had nothing to lose!!!

However, as quickly as the urge came, it faded, and Giovanni was able to regain his composure.

As JuiceBagger lay on the ground motionless, Giovanni kicked him out of the way and climbed into the driver's side of the Mazda 3i and closed the door.

All of a sudden there was a commotion in the parking lot as a little child began to point in the direction of JuiceBagger laying on the pavement.

HEY!!! DO YOU NEED HELP?!!", "HEYYYYYYY MISTER!!!!

Giovanni push started the engine, and sped out of the parking lot with a backlash of commotion and hoped like hell that the dude that he stabbed and pistol-whipped, didn't die.

If he did it was all good, but he didn't want to draw unnecessary attention to himself.

"Too late for that", he said to himself. As he came upon a red light.

He slowed down because the car in front of him had come to a complete stop. He suddenly thought about the money that was "supposedly" in the glove compartment and decided he would check to make sure.

Once the car came to a complete stop, he reached over and opened the glove compartment and instantly found a green envelope filled with dollar bills that was labeled "Expense Money".

Instantly, he was overcome with a feeling of relief because he felt that all of his problems were over. If dude died, it was for a good reason. Fuck it!

If only he realized that his life would turned into a Biggie Smalls song. "Mo Money. Mo Problems".

(Meanwhile)

JuiceBagger was fortunate to have worn his Kevlar vest under the suit that he had on. That decision saved his life tremendously. He had been having visions of trouble lately,and he had begun to wear his vest just days prior to the meeting with his clients.

As the Mazda pulled away from the scene, he was grateful that he didn't get shot. The vest wasn't a thing that he would take lightly from now on.

There was no telling whether or not his Good Samaritan was down with the opposition, so he called out to her and told her, 'I'm okay, don't worry about me."

But as he walked a couple more steps, he was overcome with pain and he passed out from the blood rush that knocked off the balance in his equilibrium.

As he regained consciousness, he was hit with the realization that he was handcuffed to a hospital bed. However, it seemed like there was nobody around. The room and the door was cracked to the extent that he noticed that nobody was posted outside either.

Unbeknownst to him, the "Detectives" that had been called to the scene by the restaurant manager, were close by. They were down the hall talking to the nurses in an attempt to sign JuiceBagger out of the hospital.

Yet, the fucked up part about it was that these weren't true "Detectives'. They were there to make sure that he didn't die. If he did, they were to dispose of the body. They were to make sure that no unwanted "heat" came back upon the Sizzler's restaurant.

The restaurant was owned by a black owner named Keith ElMore, who happened to have money to pay to see that nothing became of the situation.

His restaurant has been on the news a couple years earlier for being involved in a gang shootout in which two people were shot, one ended up being deceased on arrival to the hospital.

So for Kieth, he could not take any more chances of there being any form of news coverage about any incidents happening at his restaurant.

This was how he fed his family, and anyone taking away from his family, would be dealt with!!!

JuiceBagger looked around the hospital for something that he could use to pick the locks of the handcuffs with. But the hospital room he was in, was furnished, as bare as a babies ass.

He did not know what time it was, seeing as though he was deprived of that luxury after being relieved of his personal belongings.

"Fuck!!!" He exclaimed to himself as he thought about how he was going to find the lames who did this to him.

Because once he did, Only God knew what he was going to do to them. He was going to make them wish that that they had never met him. Because the way it stood now, only "hell" and "high waters", would stop him from making mince meat of them.

Word to the Empire!!! No Lucious Lyon shit!! This was real as real could get. He had gotten robbed for all of his shit and that didn't sit well with him at all.

He was a man who was possessed with evil thoughts. There was no such thing as taking it easy and recovering. As soon as he was mobile enough to move about the city, country, nation,planet, or wherever he needed to go, he was going to track these muhfuckas down.

He was going to be there. In the flesh!! Nothing was satiate his blood thirst for retaliation except seeing the carnage that he was capable of.

To think that he was just at painter on a canvas, was an understatement. They would see just how his skills wasn't limited to a damn piece of paper!!

He seized control of himself as he pondered how to get out of the handcuffs. Then he thought about the butterfly insignias that he were on his lapels, and said to himself, "this might work".

After struggling with the handcuffs mechanism for a while, he finally succeeded in getting the cuffs off and just like that he was free to go about his mission.

He didn't want to just walk out of the hospital room, because he did not know who was lurking outside of the door. Last thing he wanted was to run directly into the arms of nosy police officers looking to ask him a million questions.

JuiceBagger checked the window, and seeing that he was above the staff parking lot on the first floor, he opened the window and took a deep breath before leaping the four feet to the ground.

After taking a tumble like laundry in a dryer, he got up and hobbled to the first car that he saw. Luckily for him, the car was on, with the door open and keys in the ignition.

He thought to himself," Would you look at God!" And he began to smile to himself. Even though it was a Kia Sorento, he hopped behind the wheel and sped out of the parking lot like a bat in hell. He had things to do and people to see.... Lord knows... He had people to see!!!

Chapter Six

Over the next two weeks as JuiceBagger was searching for leads on who jacked him, Nouchy was taking the time to recuperate and get his priorities back in order. He had gotten a chance to get some much needed rest and relaxation as he gathered his thoughts.

JuiceBagger had called him to inform him of what had transpired and it was like a slap in the face, because he had been so adamant about Juice getting into the business venture that he was involved in.

It was a way to help one of his childhood friends get money and keep him off the streets making himself him money in the process. One hand washes the other, both hands wash the face.

Even though he hadn't been there at the meeting when JuiceBagger was robbed, he was there when the first introductions had been made.

From critiquing the character of the guys they were dealing with, Nouchy didn't think it was an inside job on their behalf. Not at all.

So he would have to figure out how this had happened, and typically, the streets would talk. So he would have to be patient until they did.

When he first was approached by Nouchy, he was hesitant to get involved. Because it meant stepping out of his comfort zone and getting involved with some high end people who would make sure they all disappeared if there was any fuckups.

This was something that he wanted to do because he needed the extra revenue. To create more for himself. He often looked to Nouchy for advice,

But on this matter, he knew that Nouchy would never ever tell someone what to do. If it involved getting money by any means necessary, he was game.

Even if he didn't himself become involved with the business venture, it was for the purpose of making headway in a world, where losers were the ones who died unknown.

People who didn't go out there and get it how they lived, ended up becoming people with nothing to live for.

Nouchy was taught to never accept losing. Nelson Mandela once said, "I never lose. I am a winner. When I win, I win. When they say that I've lost, I haven't. Losing is learning how to win. The mistakes we learn from."

After JuiceBagger had gotten released from prison for attempted murder, and drug trafficking he realized that he wanted to do something that would minimize the bullshit in his life.

Which led him to resort to the talent that he discovered that he had while incarcerated. He discovered that he could draw anything with fine detail.

His skills resembled that of being a human magnifying glass. He had to hone his skills thoroughly, but through the assistance of a institutional art class, he was able to master his craft.

Thus, giving him a new sense of direction and a chance in life once he reached the finish line of his sentence.

Once he got out he took his talents to the streets, where he made a living drawing portraits of random people on the streets.

In doing so, he created a buzz for his work that led to a chance meeting with a customer who wanted to use his skills and his eyes for making counterfeit money.

When he proposed bringing his talents to this new spectrum of living, Nouchy was initially against it but he decided that it was a chance for JuiceBagger to make his own imprint in the world. He told his fellow comrade that he gave his blessings as long as he was going to be smart about this business venture.

JuiceBagger was asked about the meeting and whether he wanted Nouchy to roll with him to see what was up. JuiceBagger told him to tag along just for moral and weapon support.

It was arranged to take place in the upscale restaurant in Soho, New York. After introductions were made and the meal had arrived and small talk passed, it was time to get down to the business at hand.

The name of the client who was making the proposal was Claude Schilling. He immediately asked the waiter to escort the party to the "Green room".

This room was located in the back of the establishment and provided a place where business could be conducted in total privacy.

Things were tense as both parties looked at each other waiting on the other to open the conversation.

Schilling took a napkin and wiped his mouth after finishing up a slice of apple pie.

He turned to look at the both of them and directed his question at JuiceBagger.

"How much do you know about counterfeiting?"

Both of them look at him and astonishment and just shrugged. It was better to say that you didn't know something, than to fake as if you knew everything and ended up making a fool of yourself.

Schilling laughed because of the total looks on their face, and said, "Okay, that's what I needed to know. Being that you don't know too much about it, I need the both of you to be patient and take in what you can. Grasp what you can. It really isn't complicated once you learn what's needed to learn in this business."

He paused as the waiter came around to offer them another round of drinks. And waited while they were distributed and she left before he continued,

"When you learn everything you need to learn, you will know what's really going on in the world. Half of the world's resources are counterfeit in one way or another."

As he kept talkin it became apparent that he was ready to talk for a lengthy amount of time. He took a sip of his drink and let it savor in his mouth as he told them," There are two sorts of counterfeiters. The bad ones and the good ones. You have to distinguish who you are, and separate yourselves. Okay?".... He paused as he waited for confirmation that he was being listened to.

After Nouchy and JuiceBagger nodded their heads, he kept going.

"Ok, now I'm going to teach you the difference between Intaglio and lithography."

He scooped a magazine off the table and handed it to them.

"Open it," he said as he allowed them to the chance to get a hands on learning experience. "You can turn to any page. Now run your fingers over the paper. It's smooth isn't it ? That's lithographic printing. That's how everything is virtually printed. Books, magazines, newspapers, and everything. What happens is that an ink roller passes over the blank paper, but intaglio is totally different."

He suddenly clapped his hands together.

CLAP!!!!

The clap caused Nouchy and JuiceBagger to jump. The sound was very loud in the quiet room. Everyone was looking in their direction. Nouchy thought to himself,"This fool tripping".

Schilling looked around the restaurant and then back at Nouchy and JuiceBagger. He apologized for the sudden outburst and said to them, "That's Intaglio. It's when a metal plate is smashed into the paper with the force of a collision. This causes it to leave a definite embossed feel to the paper. The printed image looks three-dimensional. It feels three-dimensional. It's unmistakable.

He eased his wallet from his blazer and pulled out a $100 bill. He passed it to Juice and said, Can you feel it?" After pausing to let them both feel the $100 bill, and showing them what he was trying to teach them, he continued on with what he was saying.

"The metal plate or nickel coated with a substance called Chromium. Fine lines are engraved into the Chromium and the lines are filled with ink. The plate hits the paper and the ink is printed onto do its top most surface. Understand ?"

After false nods of approval he felt comfortable to go.

" Ok. The ink is in the valley of the plate, so it's transferred to the ridges on the paper. Intaglio printing is the only way to get that raised imprint. The only way to make the forgery feel right. Its how the real thing is done".

JuiceBagger thought of a question and suddenly asked, What about the ink? Can you explain how that varies?".

Schilling was in admiration of the young man in front of him. He had heard about him from his wife, after she had gotten a portrait done by him.

He loved someone who paid attention to detail and someone who was an avid learner. He could tell from this meeting that the kid in front of him would be an asset to what he was looking to accomplish.

He took another sip of his Chardonnay before continuing, " Okay there are three colors. Black and two different kinds of green. The back of the bill is printed first with the darker green. Then that paper is left to dry. On the next day, the front is printed with the black ink. That ink is allowed the time to dry and then the front is printed again with the lighter green."

He held out the $100 bill and began to point to places on it. "That's the other stuff you see there on the front including the serial number. But the lighter green is printed by a different process called letterpress. But don't worry about that, all I need you to do is to be our engraver. I need your eye for detail and what you possess in terms of the way you pay attention to detail."

Nouchy excused himself to go smoke a cigarette. He thought to himself"Damn this muhfucka talking bro head off!" But he knew it was for a good cause, so he rolled with the punches like a boxer who knew that they was in for a hell of a right hook if they didn't duck.

When he came back to the table, the deal had been made and JuiceBagger was now in the engraving business with an opportunity to make some "Moulan Rouge AKA Pesos Dinero."

It was just what the team needed. However Nouchy didn't really have a cause or need for the money because he believed in playing fair.

Which brought him back to his present situation at hand and the fact that JuiceBagger was about to go on a rampage, if he didn't calm him down.

However, Nouchy felt that he wasn't in the frame of mind to be giving advice as of yet. He was still a mess when it came to his mental status and how he was going to go about handling things.

Sensing that K Rouga knew about all of his other places of residence, he decided to travel to one of his vacation Lodges located in Stowe, Vermont.

The weather did not add any comfort to the pain that he was faced with, as the healing process had begun, but it was a welcome change of scenery.

It was amazing how much a person could accomplish when they had time to relax their mind, body, and soul.

Nouchy had been off the grid for these past two weeks of R&R. No phone, no tablets, no other communication devices. He had even postponed the meeting with the district leaders in his organization.

It wasn't the right time to apply pressure in the streets. Even though the mere act of turning the other cheek would bring forth rebellion in his organization.

He knew how to stoke the fire if it became too rambunctious. He was more than capable of snuffing out a flame that needed to be put out.

He did not tolerate any forms of insubordination from anyone!!!!

To reach the heights of success Nouchy had to do things that made the streets respect him. standing a 5 ft 7 and 1/2, only 130 pounds soaking wet, with a couple rocks in his pocket, he had tattoos on his neck to represent his clique chain Chain Gang Empire.

He was a force to be reckoned with. He was dark skin with nappy hair. A couple people referred to him as a broke down Tyson Beckford. While at the same time calling him baby Tyrese, because of his singing abilities.

He could sing the feathers off any bird, and could sing the panties off of any sized woman. While his baby face made him attractive to many of his female acquaintances, he was also capable of transforming into someone who had fire in his eyes.

However he had long ago given up the notion of having a main lady or a main squeeze because of the business he was involved in.

The streets took no hostages and everyone who was important to you was fair game. The last thing he ever wanted was a situation where someone could use his loved ones as a form of securing whatever they wanted from him.

He didn't want to go through the process of finding someone and making their family bear the sins of the cross for any type of transgression that was committed by their family member.

He was capable of protecting himself because he was trained in the art of Tae Kwon Do. He had also been able to go to an after-school program at the PAL, also known as the Police Athletic League.

The league was established by police to give back to the community, and to let kids to go there after school to do homework and play sports. They were able to do anything positive. They even offered music classes.

The music classes offered everything that Nouchy needed in order to step his musical genius up to the next level.

When it came to the protection of his family he left that to Rozay and the rest of the security that he hired.

Rumors had been spread that Rozay was the best of the best. He had never lost anyone on his watch.

Which reminded Nouchy of the movie The bodyguard. In which Kevin Costner made it his duty to protect Whitney Houston from the stalker she had. If only they could have protected Whitney from herself.

Word had spread that Rozay was a licensed hitman. Whatever that meant. It was crazy to see how the story spread from truth, to half truth,to two fourths truth, to a total lie, real quick.

While Rozay never gave any fire to the substance of the rumors, he never denied it either.

Rozay had told him that he had learned everything from his father who served under the leadership of capable leaders who had no issue with following orders as well as issuing them.

That's what led Rozay to be able to do what he did when it came down to the protection detail.

He had to be able to sustain and maintain communication on all levels and aspects or else his leadership would be in constant threat of a mutiny.

Something that would be nipped in the bud like a flower that was about to die ASAP.

Nouchy never knew his real father and he didn't get the chance to spend that much time with Frederick. Yet, he didn't mind the madness at all because he knew what was at stake and he was above spending time dwelling on the past.

Which brought him to the sound of the phone ringing with an ordinary ringtone, but he knew who it was without glancing at the phone.

He had received two missed calls from Malachi and told had told Malachi to call him back at a designated time so they could chat. Nouchy answered the phone as he yawned at the same time.

"Yoooooo," he said until the phone.

" What up little brother?" Malachi returned the greeting.

"What's good with you my G ? You going to dinner nowadays ? Because I know that I keep your books straight.... You need some more Fettuccine Alfredo?"

Malachi laughed into the phone as he replied," You know I'm always Gucci bro. Everything I do, I do for a reason and a purpose. I only went to the cafeteria so I could pick up those phones you had mailed to old boy people for me. We was fortunate enough to get them joints past the damn police. You know how that is. You know how that goes. You win some. You lose some.

I also got some drugs in here also. I meant to tell you that I'm in the pharmaceutical business right now. I only sell to white people though. Money on the would make the day go good . You feel me ?" Nouchy replied," Most Def big bro. What up tho? Cause I know you don't call ya little brother unless you need a ear, or you need a billion dollars. So what you need?"

Malachi felt the vibes. He didn't want to be on his "Contraband" cell phone for too long anyways, so he just dived into the reason why he was calling his brother.

" I need for you to tell me that you are going to do something about that knucklehead brother of ours for shooting you".

That comment took Nouchy by surprise because he had kept that info close to his heart like the handkerchief in the breast pocket of his suit.

He gained composure of himself and said I to the phone," Damn bro how do you even know about that ? I purposely didn't tell you because I don't need you worrying about me. I can't have you shadowing me and questioning my judgment. You did make me a better person, but it's certain things that have to be done without it being done prematurely." Nouchy hesitated for a minute before continuing,

"Plus, my moms is super sick. You of all people should know that I'm capable Malachi. I'm not just about to do what everybody thinks I should do. Because it's what they would do. That's what makes me my own person."

Malachi was incensed at the way that Nouchy was acting so nonchalant about the situation. He was going to go off on his protege, but he wasn't the one with the bandages on his body to prevent blood from spilling and soaking into his clothes, so he instead said,

" I know you are capable bro. I'm not every going to question your strategy. I'm just a little thrown off by the way that you have matured. Because by now, the old you would have been put fire to K Rouga. But anyway, the little nigga comes up here to visit me,smelling like a liquor distillery, and he basically asked me what he should do about the situation."

Nouchy laughed at himself as Malachi continued, " I told him that I wasn't going to involve myself in that. The Niger bought me some food and then walked out on the visit without saying a word. That shit had me so upset that I fucked around and gave all that shit away. I need you to slap his ass for me. Ungrateful bastard!!!"

Nouchy began to laugh out loud as he struggled to envision the sight of what Malachi was telling him.

"Haha you gotta be kidding bro. I'm not even surprised he did no shit like that. That nigga has gotten too big for his baby diapers. So he think he is a grown ass man. You know about him shooting me. But you don't know why."

Malachi found himself caught up in a whirlwind of emotions and told Nouchy," Welllllllll, are you going to tell me or do I have to get a psychic to let me know what I need to know."

Nouchy shot back" You know damn well them psychic people rip you off real quick. You can't get shit done by talking to them. All they want is your credit card info so they can scam your ass and make a killing."

Malachi couldn't help but to laugh to himself as he told Nouchy" You dead right fool. But do tell me what's up. I wanna know what the fuck happened."

" Oh okay you busy as always huh ? Nouchy told him in a teasing manner. "You must have one of them big booty bunnies around there who hungry huh? Hahahaha.... "

Malachi began to tell him to shut up and get on with what he was trying to tell him, but before he could get in his retort Nouchy continued,

"Anyway, I ended up deading his ass in my organization because the nigga has divided loyalties. Remember I told you that we was taking a trip to South Carolina, to get rid of some shit with JuiceBagger and to get some yoppas from the Belliano motherfukers ?"

Malachi replied ,"Yeah I remember bro.

Nouchy began to light up a cigarette and then because to continue," That was around the time that my moms had the stroke. So I ended up letting the nigga handle the trip on his own because I wanted to be around ma.

I let JuiceBagger do something else at the time cuz I didn't know what the fuck he would do to K Rouga in my absence. You know them two fools don't get along on any level. So I had to separate them. Anyway you know her condition was critical and she wasn't expected to make it. The nigga really ain't care cuz that ain't his mom's.

So long story short, this nigga comes back with the excuse that he was robbed for the bread by some niggas in Brooklyn and he didn't have a fuckin bruise,scratch, or nothing on his ass. He was looking at me super fuckin crazy like he knew, I knew he was lying, and he wanted to see if I was going to flip out on his ass.

I kept it cool though. I didn't even trip. I told him it was cool, and I even gave him ten bands to get back right."

Malachi stopped him and said," Why the fuck you didn't smoke his ass right then and there bro? You are going to end up opening yourself up for other motherfukers to start playing with your money."

Nouchy thought for a minute as he now regretted not smoking Rouga when he played on fucked up the first time.

He replied", You are absolutely right bro. You know that I give people the benefit of the doubt. You know that anybody can come to me and get anything that they need. You know that this whole operation came to me through pops. Pops gave this nigga his life insurance policy cuz he knew he wasn't a street nigga. You feel me. So I didn't know what was up."

He took a moment to finish smoking good cigarette before continuing,

"You know that this whole operation was built from the death of our father. His blood had to be shed for our moms to get that money from her wrongful death lawsuit. This was built by family. For family. Just like FUBU. For Us By Us. I gave Rouga everything bro. You know that even though you've been locked up all these years, you've been here for him too. Not to mention that after I gave him the ten grand for that fake-ass robbery, I ended up going into the safe that I had installed in the safe house and I was missing 20 additional racks. Small enough to go unnoticed but I had counted the bread the night before. That bread had to go to the Belliano family for the weapons and the shit that they was supplying us with. I had to go to the bank and get 12 racks out of the bank.

You know I don't hold cash in the other spot.

Malachi thought about it for a second and asked," What made you feel like Rouga took that bread ?"

Nouchy replied," Bcause he was the only one with the code to the safe and he started to get beside himself by splurging in the strip club. Just doing stupid shit. So I cut him off and told him that he wasn't welcome at any of my establishments. You know I own a little car wash, I own a barbershop, and I'm enrolled in Virginia college to become a certified tax accountant. So I can learn how to wash money. I want to open a club but it's so much shit going on that I'm going to wait on that."

Malachi began to feel himself getting angry for what his brothers were going through because he was not out there physically in the flesh to protect them.

He asked Nouchy," So tell me what you are going to do about getting shot. Please don't tell me that you are going to let things go. Don't tell me you getting soft on me."

Nouchy stated to laugh, "Haha.. ouch.. Damn this fuckin sling is irritating," he said before snatching the arm sling off of his shoulder. He had injured his arm after falling in the shower while trying to take a shower in his own.

He continued, "Damn you know that Im far from soft. This situation is just so fucking awkward, so I'll just tell you that I'm going to do what is in my best interests. Seems like everybody wants to make me shoot my flesh and blood. At the same time, I'm not going to explain myself and tell you something because shit happens.

I can't expect to do something and give you my word, but then something else happens that forces me to react like a total asshole and you will be feeling some type of way because I gave you my word and didn't hold true to it. You know me and how I respond to situations, but this is different. I've never had to go against the grain. But I guess we have to experience all types of things in this lifetime. So all I can tell you is that I will make the appropriate decision, and I will not allow anything to deter me from doing the right thing."

Malachi had heard enough and it was time to get off the phone because it was about to be count time, where the officers would come around to do the evening head count.

Malachi told him," Lil bro I trust that you will do the right thing. But I want you to realize that shit is real. Your Martin Luther King approach is what you have decided to do. At the same time it may come a time when you have to transform into Malcolm X you dig. I myself, wouldn't trust the level of instability that Rouga possesses. I know what envy and jealousy can do to people. It will bring out the beast in people and make them do things they wouldn't normally do. Bitch niggas become killers, snakes become vipers, loyalty becomes disloyalty, all things to take on a different meaning. You must never forget that you have alot to lose and if you don't fight for it, then it will be taken from you without any repercussions. That's how people will feel. I'm not telling you that it needs to be something done, but it would be smart to consider it, because he will continue to play on your method of compassion and take that as weakness. I've taught you a lot young lad. I told you to always display strength. Never allow your most trusted associate to see you when you are weak.

A leader must always show strength in action strength in inaction, strength in the ability to conquer with and without war. The blood of the family has been shed ever since our birth and with the death of our beloved father, whom you've never gotten to fully enjoy, your blood is being shed in vain."

Malachi was looking outside his cell and saw that the officer would be coming around to count soon so he continued,

"You must put a end to that. Well, that's the end of my lecture. On another note I do need like $400 for the spring packages. I'm trying to get my food all of the way up.

Nouchy took in all of the wisdom that was being offered and replied," Say no more. I'm going to do that when I get off the phone. I'll end up sending you $700 this week and $700 next week. Let me know what else you need."

After the conversation was over Nouchy turned off his phone and lay back in the "Maybach" as referred to his recliner as. He was super tired and really didn't even want to be bothered right now. He needed to think to himself and "De-Stress" real quick. Little did he know he would be stressed right back out as soon as he turn the phone back on............

Chapter Seven

The last two weeks had been two weeks of pure drama for K Rouga. The ups and downs of life. The constant reminders of disloyalty, that came up in discussions of others when talking about the situation with Nouchy.

He had been emotionally and physically drained as he looked forward to the days ahead. He had a lot of work to accomplish in the streets and just wanted to relax and be through with all of the drama.If only it was so simple.

Unfortunately things didn't always work out like that. Not to mention the fact that he happened to put himself in harms way for shooting his brother.

In his mind it was all good though. Shit happened. He didn't mind the wrath of his brother. It wasn't as if he would do anything anyway.

Plus he had connects with the network that would ensure his safety and whatever he needed, whenever he needed it. So it wouldn't be hard to tip the scales in whatever direction he needed it to be in. Fuck his brother.

The scheme with the cars went off without a hitch, and he had been chosen to be one of the ones who went to the chop shop to break the cars down.

One of the Maybach Landaulet's and one of the Bugatti Veyron's were scheduled to get chopped up. These were the only two cars out of the whole bunch that was to be chopped.

Only because they had bad vehicle identification numbers, which meant that other agencies had access to those numbers.

Those cars were involved in a multi-agency operation, that required the original paperwork to be shared with other agencies even though the cars were in the property of the Bureau.

The cars were thought to have been used to traffic drugs, and even though none had been found in the car at the time of arrest, they were still impounded.

Virtually everything that had to do with illegal activities, the Network had their hands in on it.

So it was no surprise that they owned their own chop shop.

The chop shop was so create creatively designed, that it could pass as an auto body shop to anyone who came stumbling upon the location. The shop was adjacent to a car wash also.

A lot of traffic passed through the shop, and it was easy to find a nice spot to relax in the luxurious cafe that was developed for the purpose of keeping customers from being too nosey.

During the process of the Bugatti being chopped up, there was a secret compartment. Inside the secret compartment there was a secret stash of "Goodies" that K Rouga found.

Altogether, there was 10 kilos of cocaine, 50 thousand dollars in cash,along with twelve Pirelli P4 Storm Pistols.

It came as a shock to K Rouga that the feds had allowed such a find to go unnoticed or undetected.

But he realized that most likely, all the feds were after was a conviction, and maybe one of the agents had this car on a list to utilize for personal use, once the investigation and trial was over.

Since it was only K Rouga, and the employers who worked on the car, on the scene when the discovery was made, it was agreed upon that they could keep four of the pistols, Ten Grand and three kilos of cocaine.

As soon as K Rouga picked up a kilo of cocaine, he felt a rush of adrenaline as he looked at the green :-) emblem, that was emblazoned on the plastic wrap that concealed the cocaine.

After the job was done and the other employees went on lunch breaks, everyone else involved in this small wheel of fortune took turns sampling the cocaine.

From the first snort K Rouga felt a feeling of euphoria that overwhelmed him as he screamed jubilantly,

"Hell motherfucking yeah baby this that shit right here."

SNIFFFFFFFF SNIFFFFFFFFFF

He let the drain from the cocaine slide down his throat as he said to nobody in particular.

" Damnnnnnnnnn this shit fireman status".

He was Seven kilos strong, 8 Beretta's lock and loaded, and forty racks headed in the wrong direction!!!

Life was sweet. Nothing like a sweet victory to boost his morale and give him a reason to breathe easier.

Hell, for a kilo, a crackhead would take care of all of his problems with Nouchy.

He smiled to himself as he thought about life... life life...

He was in such a daze that all he could hear was the word life reverberating in his mind.

He couldn't take that lightly! Here he was with his mind and body on automatic pilot status while his beloved mother was on her deathbed.

"What?! Wait a minute. Did you just call that bitch your mother?" he heard a voice in his head say to him.

"That bitch ain't my mother. That's Nouchy's mother", he responded to the voice and continued saying," You can say that's like my mother. She's helped raise me to the point I'm at right now. Suddenly he was overcome with emotions as he was hit with the feeling that he needed to go and see his mother.

He felt in his soul, that this was the moment that he needed to go and let her know that he loved her.

Yeah, that was it !

It was now or never.

" Yo is y'all motherfuckers done snorting up all that cocaina?" , He asked the mechanics as he began to pace and move around the shop.

" I got some shit to do. And no time to spare. So I'll tell y'all what I'm going to do."

He explained that he was leaving the drugs, guns, and money at the shop, and he needed them to make a spot in his Mercedes Benz C L A 45 AMG, to hold the drugs guns and money for him.

He told them that he would have his people's come pick up the car when they were done.

He agreed to give them an additional kilo, two more guns and $7,500 more in cash.

He knew that they would play fair because this was a spot owned by the network, and they wouldn't be alive for two seconds if they played the game like Cam Newton in the 2015 super bowl against Denver !

A Rich had a relationship with the owner of the shop so if anything ever went wrong, then heads would roll, and shit would roll downhill to all of their families.

They were trustworthy though. There wasn't a lot of doubt in his mind that they were concrete. He knew they could be counted on to be efficient and loyal, to the dollar signs that they were just awarded with.

The mechanic allowed K Rouga to use his car in order to do what he needed to do. All K Rouga had to do was be careful not to fuck up the car.

It was a classic royal blue 1976 Corvette stingray, with over $20,000 invested in the transformation of the interior and exterior.

From the V8 engine, to the sound system, to the vinyl ragtop that covered the top of the car, to the rear suspension and transmission, and the Continental White Wall Tires. However, K Rouga could care less about that bullshit.

All he knew was that he needed to go see his mother now !!!!

The traffic was light as he sped uptown to the hospital located in the upper Bronx on 161st Street.

Literally around the corner from the beloved home stadium of the New York Yankees.

As he pulled up to the hospital, he pulled out a pair of Aviator sunglasses, that happened to be in the arm rest of the driver seat.

He was attempting to hide the redness in his eyes that had emerged as a direct result of the drugs he had consumed at the shop.

He took one last snort of the product that he kept for his personal stash.

He began to let the drug stream down his nostrils, as he was once again hit with a one-two combination from the coke gods.

SNIFFFFFFFF SNIFFFFFFFF

He sucked up all the extra snot and cocaine, as he exited the vehicle and slamed the door shut, forgetting that the keys were in the ignition.

" Damn this cocoa butter on fleek !", he said to himself as he thought, "This shit is like fine wine. It gets better with time. I'm going to enjoy this shit."

As he walked toward the hospital entrance, he could feel every iota of air that brushed across his face. He could he ever hear every bird singing Sweet songs. Every horn blasting out its own melody. Every person laughing, talking, enjoying life.

He entered the lobby and immediately saw a familiar face. The nurse who had flirted with him on a few occasions. She saw him at the same time and spoke first,

" Hello mister, I haven't seen you in a few days but yet, you remind me of a good song. You get lost over time until someone reminds you that you need to make an appearance. What's the word, bird ?"

He smiled as he replied," I've been busy tying up a few loose ends that my mom's would have wanted to get done. How is her prognosis anyway ?"

"Baby its still day-to-day. Every minute and second count, but I'll tell you this, your mom's is a fighter. I know that you already know that so it ain't no need to stress that, but as of 12 hours ago the doctors changed her status to stable condition.

So that means that she is on the road to recovery. She still can't breathe on her own, but she will be okay once her lungs get to working."

K Rouga was surprised at the news and even smiled to himself, thank the spirits for miracles.

He looked at the nurse with a faint look of admiration as he asked her, " Do you think that I can see her real quick."

Although Kamara didn't want to let him in , she could not resist after she looked into his eyes. Oh God, how he made her panties wet.

"You know it's after visitation hours, I could lose my job behind letting you go in to see her. But I'll do you this favor, if you do me a favor in turn."

K Rouga already knew where this was leading because he had studied the Art Of Seduction by Robert Greene. He knew she was going to ask for something sexual. But wanting to make her say it, to stroke his ego he replied,

"What is that favor?"

He knew that the look in her eyes. It had all the signs of sexual lust and the thirst and hunger for a good strong serving of meatballs. His meat and his balls!!

"Let me suck that dick of yours sometime soon. I've been wanted to let you sample this pussy but I'll accept a slurpee for right now. I want to see what flavor it is. What you say to that ? "

K Rouga's dick got hard just from the thought of the dirty proposition. He grabbed his dick as he read her name tag.

"Well Miss Kamara, I will gladly accept. As a matter of fact, here is my number. Hit me up when you get off work, and we can arrange that composition of sweet music right away. I love to collaborate."

Kamara replied in a slutty voice ,"I damn sure do to baby. Now go ahead and see your mother while nobody is looking. I'll be out here."

After giving her his number he said" I'll be out in a few."

He made his way to the third floor and the last door on the end. The woman who had "helped raise his brother" was the second person in the bed farthest to the wall.

There was a sectional curtain that could be used to divide the room for privacy, so he pulled the curtain back and stared at his brother's mother.

The swelling in her face had went down considerably and her facial color had returned to its natural color. Instead of the purplish bluish color that had gripped her body when this first happened.

K Rouga hated the way she looked but he also knew that it was human nature to live and die and all that other unfortunate shit in between. He was accustomed to the smell of the antiseptics, and all the other chemicals used to sterilize the hospital where disease was rampant in so many ways.

His thoughts faded to a few distant memories of his childhood. There were good times and moments when he was the focus of his Felicity's affections. He relished those moments.

Then there were times when her affection was null and void like a bad check. It was these times, that she shared with P Nouchy. Just the thought of Nouchy, brought anger to K Rouga's soul as he stared at his brother's mother laying in a hospital bed looking so serene and peaceful.

He was overcome with thought of his own mother's voice speaking to him in his mind taunting him.

" You need to be like your brother. He will become somebody in this life and you need to decide what you are going to do."

He also heard her say," Why can't you be like your brother ? He gets good grades in school. Why can't you be like your brother ? He wears decent clothes. You look like a hoodlum. "

K Rouga was always compared by his mother to Nouchy even though their mothers didn't get along at all and his mother had limited contact around Nouchy.

No matter what he did, Nouchy did it better. His own mother's affection had them like a light with no flame.

Looking down at Nouchy's mother, his mind began playing tricks on him, and he was overcome with feelings of disgust towards her.

He looked at her and said, "You don't know who the fuck I am do you ?! I'm K motherfucking Rouga. You made me who I am and you gave me to the streets when that bitch ass son of yours came calling. When I needed you you wasn't there. Where was you ?......"

K Rouga was a man possessed by intoxicants and there was no controlling him. He continued to spew hatred at Felicity through his words as he continued on his rant.

"Wellllllllllll...... let's see..... You was with Nouchy! Always kissing him and praising him. Where the fuck is he at now?! Tell me that you old bitch. You can't hear me talkin to you? Huh ?"

At that moment he had gone from the bowels of sanity to the trenches of Loonyville.

He allowed the cocaine to possess him as he continued on.

" I know you ain't disrespecting the Rouga man. Maybe if I take that cord out of your mouth you will be able to talk. Or better yet how about this !" He snatched the plug to the oxygen machine, out of the electrical socket, as he began to pace and walk beside her bed.

He looked at her he felt no emotions but hatred for her and hatred for her bastard son. He wanted to make sure that they knew his name and he wouldn't stop until they did.

"In a few seconds your ungrateful ass will be dead and can't nobody help you, you old piece of pussy."

He lifted up her hospital gown and slid her panties down as he stuck his finger in her pussy and sniffed it.

He frowned up his face and said," Damnnnnnnn your pussy stink. Your pussy on twang right now. I should fuck you to death and watch you take your last breath you ungrateful whore. I should fuck you how you did me when you chose Nouchy over me. But I don't have time right now. Haha just like you!!!?? There are more important things I have to attend to if you knew what I mean."

He noticed that her chest was still rising despite her not being hooked up to the machine. He thought to himself, "This bitch can breathe on her own and I thought this shit was going to be easy." He walked around the curtain, and removed a pillow from the empty bed next to the door, and walked around and placed it over her face.

Felicity knew that something was wrong with her when she could no longer feel the whoosh of air flowing through her air channels. That was the only thing that had saved her senses. Even though she was in a drug-induced coma, she still heard everything K Rouga had been saying to her. She couldn't remember any memories while in this state of subconsciousness but she also knew that she could not breathe all of a sudden. It was it a bad thing that she couldn't breathe. She knew she was in a hospital. Why didn't the doctor help her breathe?! Damn!! As she was getting weaker by the moment, all she could feel was the choking sensation that enveloped her and she knew she was being suffocated. She also knew why. She hoped to God that he would accept her as she was. She had had a long life and had suffered too many times not to be accepted at the pearly Gates. She also hope that K Rouga would find peace within but most of all , she hoped that her death did not happen in vain. Her final thoughts were cut short as she felt her life drain from her and was engulfed in brightness.

The wails of the machine snapped Kendrick from his trance as he quickly removed the pillow and raced to the plug in the oxygen machine.

He placed the breathing cord back into her mouth, and was moving to put the pillow back in place as an orderly ran into the room and looked him up and down.

As she asked him" what the hell happened",

he looked at her with a false sense of exasperation and said,"

I don't know I was looking out of the window when the alarms went off. Can you tell me what that sound means?" K Rouga responded while trying hard to suppress a laugh inside his chest.

"It means that your loved one is in a cardiac arrest and needs help. You need to leave her side before the doctors come rushing in here asking questions.

K Rouga, in a perverse way of thinking, gave Felicity a kiss on the lips and whispered in her ear, "Sleep in Peace bictch", before he exited the room still holding the pillow.

Instead of returning the way he came in at, he wandered out of a side door and was shocked by the sight of the Corvette being gone from the spot he parked it at.

"Ain't no way in the fuckin hell", he exclaimed as he raced up and down the parking lot, in the hopes that he maybe was just tripping off of what had just happened, and he had possibly parked the car in a different spot.

After 5 minutes of looking like a chicken with his head chopped off, he raced to a car that had just dropped off a pregnant woman and her husband. He ran out to the car and snatched open the door preparing to give whoever it was in the car, a "bad day", when he heard a voice say," HEY YOU!!!! STOP RIGHT THERE!!! "

At first glance he looked back and saw that it was a hospital security guard, so he continued what he was in pursuit of doing until the guard said,

"That's it buddy you asked for it."

He started to throw the man out of the car but realized that he would never make it in time before the guard caught up to him.

He didn't want anything to trace him back to the hospital, knowing that Kamara couldn't say anything about his surprise visit.

So he began to run towards the train station located four blocks away, praying that whoever this dude was he didn't try to be a fuckin hero. Because heroes ended up like Malcolm X, Martin Luther King Jr, Tookie Williams, OG Mack and countless others. QUITE DEAD!!!!

Jon Belliano was in law school, and he was also working as a security guard to help pay for the law books, time, and respect of other lawyers, and a sense of direction to his daily life.

Even though his family was more than "well-off", he did not want to be known as," The Mobsters Son" all of his life, so he had taken his education seriously and had the drive to work towards one day being recognized for who he was as a person, not who his father was.

He had taken the initiative to go to school diligently and truly dedicated his time to studying and becoming a lawyer. In his father's circle of friends, there was always a demand for a good lawyer.

How ironic it would be if there came a time where he had to defend his father in a case. That would be very good. " Mobster defended by son!" or Son of Mob on the Job!!" the newspapers would love it up.

To pay for law school he would not do it with any money financed by the mob, so he worked his ass off at the hospital.

He was on break smoking a cigarette when he came across the precarious situation with a black dude try to jack a car from a white dude.

All of a sudden the dude took off running like a cheetah in chase of a meal.

He looked down and saw his feet moving too. He chuckled inside. hahaha.. he was accustomed to having blackouts which was why he kept his pills in his pocket. But he couldn't get to them now. Not while he was performing the task of fighting crime.

K Rouga waited in the alley of the lot where he knew the fat guy with pass by in pursuit of a suspect he was trying to apprehend.

K Rouga heard his breathing before he came and was ready for his next move. He reached in his pocket and pulled out the fixed blade knife made by LaRue tactical. He snapped open the blade which was 10 inches long.

"Damned if you do.. Damned if you don't." he said as he waited until they dude was right up on the alley.

He waited until he was a couple feet away and stuck his arm out and clotheslined him with a clothesline that would make a Ray Lewis jealous!!!!

BOOOOOOMMMMMMM!!!!!!

As the dude fell K Rouga grabbed his shirt collar and dragged him in the alley.He wasted no time on attacking his prey. He was a lion in heat!

He thrust downwards on the top of the skull with the knife that was designed for carving up kill, out on the range in the wilderness.

So he knew that it would break through the seal of a human's cranium. As knife met his cranium, K Rouga quickly kicked him off of the knife, and bent down to meet him as he struggled to stand up.

He thrust upward with the blade pointing to his rib cage section as he clamped down on the mouth of the unsung hero.

His aggression returned full force as he pulled the blade out of the rib cage area and quickly slicef the windpipe of his new victim.

"Whoooooooo", he yelled in jubilation." I can get accustomed to this shit right here. Better than doing drugs." He thought to himself.

With that done he threw his victim to the ground and commenced to stabbing him multiple times. He was going to make sure this motherfucker was dead. Cocksucka!!!!

With every entry and exit of the knife Jon knew that his life was over and there was nothing that he could do about it.

He tried to ask why, but was rewarded with a poke right in his mouth.

What was ironic about the whole situation was that if he hadn't went out to smoke those godforsaken cigarettes he would be alive come tomorrow morning.

But that would not be the case. His mother had warned him that his beloved cigarettes would be the death of him. How true it was, he thought to himself as he felt himself choking on his own blood.

"Ahghg ahghgh... why... why..."

K Rouga got up from the victim of his newfound hobby and look down on him as he spoke,

"You were in the way, now you have been removed just like a gall stone in my bladder. You ain't dead yet hahaha. At least you will be able to look over your family when you get to where your motherfucking ass going. When you get up that bitch, tell that bitch Felicity I said what's up. Until then, I'm out of here like a homerun player."

With that he was in the wind. The blood that had soaked up his pants had turned his black pants, purple and black. Still, it was nighttime and anyone passing by would think his clothes were dark. He couldn't move on without doing one more thing. Something that would save his life at least for now....

Chapter Eight

After doing a mini workout that involved doing push-ups and crunches and other activities that helped him work out his abdomen area, Nouchy jumped into a steaming hot shower in order to remove the tenseness from his mind, body, and soul.

So much of his life had been consumed by fires of adversity that he was scarred for life. At the same time his knowledge on certain things had evolved into maturity allowing him to be equipped and diverse in his rationalization of situations.

It was 11:45 p.m. when he decided to retrieve his cell phone and turn it on. A few hours had passed by and he knew that he would be bombarded with calls, texts, and messages from everybody and their mama.

It was times like this that he longed for a normal life. How good it would feel to be able to relax from the constant pressures of being in the streets, and the pressure of life on both fronts.

The joys of life is what compelled him to continue his efforts to ensure that his family, immediate and adopted, never wanted for anything.

But those expectations and successes came with prices to pay. Because the streets didn't care about anything except getting a piece of the pie. No matter how you look upon the situation. Either you gave it to the streets, or you gave it to God. Not in a spiritual way either.

Either you gave the essence their just due, or you became a statistic of circumstance.

Nouchy lit up a blunt of Balla Berries, mixed with some Og Runtz. A new grade of fire weed that had lil homies in the Bronx supplied him with.

"Swoooooooooo.....hiss, hiss..". he inhaled on the potent Mary j Blige and began to scroll down his call log and was surprised that only a few people called him.

He didn't think anything of it because he knew that if one of his peeps called him and didn't get an answer after three tries, it would mean that he was off the grid and that would be relayed so others wouldn't waste time trying to reach him in vain.

He scrolled to his text messages and saw that he had messages from Keke.

Keke: Bro where you at ?(7:45 p.m.)

Keke: EMERGENCY!!!!!!! (8:10 p.m.)

Keke: Pick up the phone!!!! (8:12 p.m)

Keke: Your Momma just died. :-((8:15 p.m.)

Keke: I need you to get to the hospital ASAP. I'm losing it I need you bro please hurry. (8:18 p.m.)

Keke : What are you doing ? !!! (8:20 p.m.)

Keke : Where you at bro ? (8:23 p.m)

Nouchy was hit with a strong feeling of grief and sadness as he scrolled down the messages seeing that his sister was the only one of his family who had attempted to call or text him.

He immediately grabbed his gun and jacket off the ottoman in the foyer and headed out the door with tears in his eyes.

"Ain't no way in hell, this can't be true". He said to himself, as he ran to the black Dodge Durango and jump into the driver seat and hit the start button to crank the truck up.

After that, it was a blur to him as he sped down highway after highway, speeding through traffic lights, and ignoring the protest of other drivers as well as pedestrians.

A part of him was gone, never to return again. Gone too soon. Even though he had expected the result to happen eventually, it shouldn't have come to this. Not with the prognosis that the doctors had given his mother a few days ago. it was something that didn't make sense.

Amidst a barrage of crazy thoughts,emotions, and impulses Nouchy finally made it to the hospital parking lot, and parked in the first lot that was open. He immediately ran into the open doors and was met by his Keke who was pacing back and forth in the waiting room.

No words were exchanged as they embraced each other and held on to each other.

Nouchy knew that he needed to be strong in order to console his family and be the Patriarch that his mother could no longer be. Nouchy allowed himself and his childhood friend to share the embrace for five long minutes, and then he began to pull himself together.

There were things that had to be taken care of. The funeral arrangements had to be made and a couple of other things had to fall into place. Which meant that he had to be active in the process of all of this because he knew that Keke would be of no use to him at all.

She was going through more grief than him it seemed, and it was not even her mother that had succumbed. He was grateful for her being able to get to the hospital and she was there for almost a day and a half before Nouchy had gotten the messages.

He forced himself to get himself emotionally detached from the situation at hand. He would allow himself to fully grieve later on after this mess was taken care of. But for right now, his mind needed to be focused.

He turned to Keke and spoke to her with concern in his voice as he told her," Take a few minutes to have a seat and relax. I'm going to have a word with the doctors and I'll be back out to take you home. I don't think that you are in any condition to drive. I know you could drive if you had to but let me take care of things for you.,"

Keke was so overcome with emotions that all she could do was nod her head in agreement at his suggestion.

Simply because she wasn't in the mood to do too much. It felt as if she had died along with Felicity. Felicity was the mother she wished she always had. Being an orphan from an early age Keke didn't really have no bad memories with her own mother because she died when Keke was 1 day old.

Felicity was always there for Keke. From day one Keke and Felicity were close. Felicity was always good to her and showed her that it was very important to always be good to people. That's why Keke became a nurse. Felicity was a human example of everything she learned in life and who she was as a person came from Felicity.

There was this one time when Keke had come home with a black eye from getting into a fight with another girl over a boy who had a crush on Keke.

The other girl was just jealous because Keke was more beautiful than she was in her popularity was up there.

Normally Keke have gotten her "groupies" to beat the bitch ass but she wanted to hit her with her own fist for the purpose of showing others that she would not be intimidated in any situation.

There would be no room for any type of weakness on her part. So she wouldn't accept being played like a sucker.

Even if she could get her own peeps to do her dirty work she felt the need to put in work. Her own work. It made her feel real and it made her grounded in reality. The reality that nobody would feel sorry for her in any way or circumstance. No matter what.

It was a world that was cold and cruel and no matter what, lines would always be drawn.

When Felicity saw her with the black eye she took her to her house and took one look at her and immediately sat her down at the kitchen table and asked her what happened.

The thing about Felicity was that she was a wise woman with more than enough stories and experiences to use to teach children with.

And there was very little that could cause her to become unhinged in any way. That would display conduct unbecoming of a lady with class.

After telling her Godmother the story Kiki waiting until her Felicity had pondered upon the situation, and she listened as Felicity told her "First off, baby there is nothing in this life that you have to prove to nobody. Especially when you have to prove yourself through violence. All of this for a little boy who ain't even going to call you tomorrow, after he find out you got your little narrow behind kicked.

The only thing that matters is your happiness and even if you want this one boy in particular, he ain't the only little boy in the school who probably like your little butt. Shoot honey, I know you can find someone who aint popular and make the best of a new acquaintance.

Its always better to have a diamond that nobody knows is there because then you can always put your own price on it, and you can always decide what it means to you. Your own value."

Keke know that Felicity was long winded like she was a saxophone player. But she will loved her knowledge and wisdom. So she kept her mouth closed as Felicity continued,

"To fight over someone who has no worth, is to fight over nothing at all. You are just fighting to say you had a fight.

I don't know who does that. But my baby doesn't need the bullshit. You got your mama's looks baby. Even if I didn't birth you. Ain't no way you fighting over a boy ! You should have them boys fighting over you. Sometimes you need to know what the fight is for and decide if the fight is going to be avoided or not".

Keke smiled to herself as she came to her senses after the daydream she had. She looked around the hospital in search of her brother and found him in an intense conversation with one of the nurses on shift, a doctor, and an orderly who was dressed in street clothes instead of Scrubs.

Although she couldn't hear what was being discussed she could tell by the reaction on Nouchy's face that he was pissed. And anybody who knew Nouchy knew that,whenever he got pissed he tended to do some crazy shit.

It was never a good sign for the motherfukers on the receiving end of his wrath. Being that they were in a hospital and she didn't want Nouchy to go "full metal jacket" in here, she decided to intervene before he did anything he would regret.

However as soon as he saw her he regained his composure and grab her by the hands as he led her away from the doctors and other prying eyes. "Let's get up out of here before I put some holes in a few of these are incompetent motherfukers. We can take my car. I'll have Tiana come get your car and take it to your crib."

Keke was looking at Nouchy because he was in one of his moods again and she wanted to know what he was talking about.

"What was you talking about with them doctors ? Because whatever the fuck they said to you, it triggered you to go off. And I need to know so I can know what to do."

Nouchy knew that what he had learned was something that was a total game changer. Yet, he didn't want anybody else to have this information because then he wouldn't have the element of surprise on his side.

So he told her," It's better that you don't know. You know that I would never hold nothing from you but at the same time I don't want to make something more bigger than what it is. If it proves to be nothing you will be the first to know. If it's something that needs to be checked then I will check it. End of story."

Kiki knew that it was no need to continue to fight for an explanation because both of them were stubborn. It wouldn't lead to nowhere but a showdown that neither of them needed right now. So she decided that she would leave it at that for right now.

But if it turned out to be something that needed to be addressed, then she would be right there, ready to bust her gun for a mother's memory. Someone would pay the price!!!!

After leaving from the scene of the murder, K Rouga got in touch with the Mexicans at the auto body shop and informed them that he would be through the shop at his earliest convenience in a couple of days.

They informed him that they would be ready for him to come and get the car in a couple of days. He told them to make sure they followed his details to the letter. He had to do some things in that car real soon.

After hanging up with them he called A Rich and got his voicemail. So he decided to call up hisother partner name Elgin. They called him L's for short.

He knew that most likely L's would have the whereabouts on A Rich. They hung out more than the rest of the click.

L's answered the phone on the first ring,

" Yoooooo what's good fool ?"

" Whats good L's ? K Rouga replied before continuing, as he rolled up a blunt.

"Have you seen A Rich bro ? I just tried to reach that fool but he ain't pull up on me yet.

" Yeah I seen A Rich, he over here with me right now. He was in the back room counting money up. You know that nigga doesn't answer the phone for his own mama when we counting up money."

K Rouga laughed out loud before telling L's,

"You know A Rich momma dead. Don't let him hear you say that shit you will be a statistic.

L's thought about that for a second and realized that what he had just said was true. Every part of it. There were 3 people in the morgue who had talking about A Rich's mother.

He told K Rouga to hold on a minute as he went to go locate A Rich.

K Rouga listened as L's could be heard in the background saying," Yo, Rouga want to bark at you real quick."

After a short delay A Rich came on the phone, "Speak and it's as instructed",

K Rouga replied," What's up big homie, I'm just checking on you and trying to figure out if you handled those things I needed you to handle for me yet.'

A Rich counted up the last pile of hundred before he responded to K Rouga." I did the first thing for you, and that should happen as we speak. So I'll check on the progress of that and let you know. As far as the other thing, I'm going to holler at them face-to-face tomorrow. You might as well come with me since this concerns you. As a matter of fact I need you to make a run with me anyways real quick. How fast can you get here ?"

K Rouga looked at his watch and said," Shidddd it's about to be 1 in the morning, so the next 4 train is at 1:18. I'll be in Brooklyn by 2. Y'all going to meet me at the train station on Fulton Ave?"

A Rich thought about it for a second before he said, "Yeah we'll be there. Make sure you dress for the rain. It might get wet."

K Rouga's ears perked up at that comment because that meant that somewhere down the line they would be putting in some work. AKA violence known as "Wet Work" it only got wet because of all the blood that would be shed.

K Rouga replied," you already know that's how I ride."

"FASHO?".

"FASHO". Put L's back on the jack real quick famo. after a minute or two L's came back on the line. "What's up fool?"

K Rouga replied," Shidddd you tell me what's up do you know where we going?"

L's didn't know what he was talking about so he said, "You obviously know more than I do because you telling me something that I didn't know. That's real talk. Bro said where we going?"

"Nigga if you don't open your ears up I'm going to fuck you up. I just told you that I didn't know where we was going. All he said was to bring my water guns, and wear my rain suit."

L's was completely thrown for a loop by that comment but he wasn't about to make Ruger aware that this news was unsettling to him. He didn't want him to hop on the phone and let A Rich know what L's thought.

L's knew that K Rouga couldn't hold water, even if the glass was glued to his hand. So instead of giving any indication on the subject, he just told Rouga,

" Ima get up with you when we get together bro .

" Say no more then, make sure you got your a game in your pocket. You might need it", K Rouga replied.

" Already". L's replied as he hung up the phone and went into the den where he had most of his clothes. He walked past A Rich who was still counting up another stack of the money that needed to go to the Belliano family.

There was nothing in his face to suggest that anything was amiss but L's knew on the contrary, A Rich was a master of disguises. A master of many faces.

He could hold his true emotions to the side while in true killer mode and nobody would be the wiser until he flipped the fuck out and went Archie Bunker's on a motherfucker.

L's also knew that anytime A Rich didn't tell you something it was for a reason. Either he was protecting your best interest or he had something close to his heart that he didn't want to share. Those were usually bad things for the people he didn't tell.

"Better safe than sorry, he said to himself as he took off his under armour shirt, and put on a BlackHawk tactical vest that was capable of withstanding a round up to 7.16 coming from a rifle.

He had gotten a lot of his gear from his cousin Lendell who was in the army. He forgot what base he was stationed at but it didn't matter to him as long as he was coming through with the tools and other knick-knacks fuck the rest.

Lendell had recently sent L's some gear that L's had kept to himself. It was no reason to let anybody know what he had going on. There was a time and place where you kept it real and where you kept it to yourself.

L's knew that he was playing with fire every time he did what he did but the pussy was too good to care about the full ramifications of his actions. Even if it was morally wrong, it was sexually right. Now he knew what R. Kelly meant when he said "My minds telling me noooooooooo, but my body is telling me yeahhhhhhhh!!!!!"

A Rich noticed a change in demeanor and in the way he change his clothes but he thought nothing of it.

It wasn't as if he knew that what was going down. He didn't have a clue. At first, A Rich was going to let him ride with the extramarital affair with his baby mother, but decided that now was the time to end all of that.

It would result in a loss of much-needed intellect on the home front, and the front lines, but A Rich was certain that K Rouga could be groomed to be the next in line. Not only was K Rouga smart but he listened to instructions.

That was a key element in the realm of leadership. Gut instincts, good listening skills. You can hear a lot of valuable information if you open your ears up to hear the peons, as well as the role-players.

Sad as it may be A Rich was tempted to let L's slide with his life but to be a boss you had to live by a certain standard, and make others live by your standards as well.

To demand respect you have to earn it, and once you earned it you had to keep it. Because if you ever lost the respect of the streets, not only would you be food for the predators, but you would be soil for the ground. Meat for the vultures. Potassium for the maggots. Flower food.

A Rich turned to L's and told him, a bro we got to drop some of this cash down on the boardwalk. Gather up the Duffies so we can split this shit up into two piles.

A Rich made up his own lingo as he went along and it was so beyond the norm that it often stuck. It was law after being said. Duffies was his way of saying duffle bags. Harriet's was his way of saying 20s referring to 20 dollar bills.

Anything you could think of he had an abbreviation for.

L's looked at A Rich to see what he was thinking, before he said, " It's almost 2 in the morning bro we've never moved this late before what's up ?"

A Rich looked at him and told him what was really up in order to ease his mind a little bit.

"I'm actually striving to test K Rouga on some wet work type shyt. I need to see where his loyalty lies. I know where your loyalty is at, but sometimes it comes to a point in time where the mantle must be passed down.

I was thinking about taking you off the streets and placing Rouga in the 1st LT spot. It takes a different kind of animal to maintain, control, and demand our dues. I've seen the best of the best deteriorate into being the ones who become the bottom of the barrel.

I've seen a hunger in Rouga's eyes as of late and it's making me lean toward giving him at least one chance to move up in the ranks. Even if it may be prematurely.

I want to move people around to where they are needed now. Not where they want to be. I need you to be in charge of my security detail. That what that way I can groom you to be the next in line to the dope game because I'm not looking to stay in this position forever.

I have better options with less stress you feel me?"

L's looked at A Rich and saw a glimpse of a smirk before his face returned to the unreadable mass that so many were accustomed to seeing.

L's knew that he had to play his part so that A Rich wouldn't be aware of the situation. Yet, L's knew that he from previous knowledge of past situations that he had to be on point so that he wouldn't be caught slippin if A Rich intended to catch him slipping.

He just nodded and said, "Im with you Rich, I have no issues with whatever you want to do. Whatever you want to accomplish I'm all for it. I don't have too much to say on the expansion of my responsibilities. However I want to choose my own people to help me protect you. I know how people can get when you have someone else step in and take over the realm on somebody else's job. I don't have time to deal with the bullshit of another person because your safety will be in jeopardy if we aren't on the same page."

A Rich went to L's and embracef him and said,

"You got it bro do you."

L's looked at him like he was crazy, but he just kept his comment to himself, as he said to himself, This nigga think I'm stupid or slow. Here he go with this Brooklyn shit trying to run game as if I'm a fuckin Monopoly board."

He felt the eerie feeling that he always felt whenever he had to put in his own wet work. Which was why he had his compact 45 caliber Para- ordnance p104 pistol, tucked under the waistline of his 511 Tactical TDU trousers.

It was just enough room in the waist that when he tucked the pistol it took away the slack, in the waist and concealed the bulge of the pistol at the same time.

L's took a moment before he said "I appreciate the upgrade and position bro. I honestly and genuinely thank you for it. Ain't shit I've seen that I can't handle, but I just feel like I want to explore more. I want to expand our operation outside of Brooklyn. The money is good, but I want the power. The respect of having niggas fearing us at an all-time high."

A Rich thought for a second before dropping wisdom on L's.

"Sometimes money brings respect, and power. Because even if you are a bitch ass nigga, if you have money then you have the streets. You have the attention of the people. You wouldn't even have to put in any kind of work, because people will kiss your ass in order to do your bidding for you. Money=power=respect what more can you want......."

L's took in the wisdom and closed his eyes and said a prayer. It was the first time that he had prayed in a long time. He prayed that his sons would cost him his life. He prayed that his life wouldn't be cut short because of his lust for some "Wet Ass Pussy" as Meg Thee Stallion said.

Either way, he was at peace with whatever happened. But he also knew that when the smoke cleared and he was alive and well, there would be hell to pay and autopsies to perform, for anybody who tried to harm him in any way.

Life would never be the same.. Not now. Not ever. And L's was totally happy with that. He had made his bed. And however it turned out, he was ready to press his luck. Or was he......

Chapter Nine

Over the past couple of weeks, JuiceBagger had made it his life's long mission to find the punk ass muhfuckas who had done the unthinkable, and robbed him for his prized possession Mazda 3i, and everything else he had in the car.

To be totally honest, it really wasn't about the car or the amount of money that he had lost out on. Because material things had no type of influence over him. Of course, like any type of civilized person with some sort of decency about themselves. He took pride in his appearances.

So, for an individual or in this case, "individuals", to intentionally oppress him of his hard earned possessions, he felt totally violated and he was going to make sure that they felt how he felt at this very moment. But he wasn't going to take their property, he was going to take their life !

This whole situation was way over the top, and these goofy's had took it upon themselvess to literally and physically deprive him of something that he had gained through his own blood, sweat,tears. He had come up in the world after coming home from prison. He had risen to the top after hard fought battles through his successes and his defeats.

But two individuals who were looking for a come up, made a decision to affect his livelihood and his whole train of thought.

JuiceBagger now understood, why the world was so full of people who committed what some would consider to be senseless acts of violence. Some would be horrified at the notion that one would be so morally inconsiderate at taking someone's life or less, as retribution for an act committed against them.

Yet even though he had risen to the top of his fortune by putting in work against other people, in his heart he felt that what he was doing, he was doing it for just cause. And that's was why he had no trouble doing so.

But in the circumstances he now found himself in, he finally knew what it was like to be the one preyed upon. The one who had been labeled as weak by an individual who really didn't know him from a can of paint.

This feeling was a feeling that brought forth emotions that would fuel a forest fire and would ignite a nuclear weapon.

So, for that small act of indiscriminate, indiscretion, on the part of these individuals, he was about to make someone's family have to grieve as the laws governed by nature took effect. Through his thorough beatdowns and physical assaults, that he put on the crackheads in the hood (who sold anything that wasn't under police protection), he had gotten a pretty solid lead about who was responsible for causing him discomfort, rib bruises, many sleepless nights.

He had a hard dick from wanting to let his hammer go and he was waiting for these goofy's outside of their reported place of refuge.

JuiceBagger had found out that the individuals responsible was a pair of troubled youths,who had caused terror on his particular section of Tremont avenue and 183rd Street in the Bronx.

J Gunna as he was referred to by the people whom JuiceBagger had spoken to, was someone who JuiceBagger immediately label as a dirtbag.

He was claimed to be an individual who took from anybody and everybody, with no regard for age, sex and ethnicity,sexual preference, religion or health status.

This J Gunna dude was someone who brought havoc to anybody that he wanted to run over, get over on, or whom he just wanted to intimidate into making them pay for what he wanted in life. JuiceBagger spoke to old woman, children, even the pastor of the local church and determined that allowing J Gunna to exit this situation with his health and life in tact would be detrimental to the welfare and well-being of so many others.

Even though JuiceBagger was a street niggga, he still advocated for the advancement and cultivation of those in the areas affected the most by the governmental lack of compassion.

Those people in the hood who, if they received honest care and attention in their communities, would gain the most from any type of sincere help from punk ass Uncle Sam.

So JuiceBagger was prepared to do what he came to do without feeling any type of remorse in his soul for this scumbag that he was about to take to the vet and have put down.

Literally, he wanted to take this muhfucka to the veterinarian and have him euthanized like the animal he was. But he knew that all things didn't go as planned. So he had a plan B. Because in his line of work, if you failed to plan you planned to fail.

Which was why he painstakingly and deliberately made it his duty to memorize every form of getaway, in case he had to make a getaway in a haste.

He had gotten to know a couple of children from J Gunna's building to serve as lookouts and to alert him when they saw this J Gunna.

At first, JuiceBagger had completely given up the notion that he would find J Gunna, because this punk ass motherfuker hadn't been to the hood to stake his claim on his self given territory in over a week.after getting the info from his informants.

But as sure as shit comes out of every creatures ass, on God's green earth, J Gunna popped his head into the hood and JuiceBagger was alerted by one of the children via text.

Chaos: Ay Juice, he's here hurry up before he goes.

To which JuiceBagger replied,

JuiceBagger: I'm on my way don't let him get out of your sight. Take a picture if you can get one without him noticing you taking one.

Chaos: Ok .

JuiceBagger peeled out of the safe house in Canarsie Queen's, jumped into the Kia Soul that he had rented for the week and was outside J Gunna's building in 45 minutes flat, after speeding through every red light as if he had a license to do so.

He chuckled to himself because he had gotten a police light that flashed blue and red lights, that he could attach to the top of his roof and it had worked like a charm. Almost too perfectly. It was as if God was on his side and the almighty wanted this to be etched in stone to happen without further delay.

JuiceBagger was interrupted by his phone vibrating with a text from Chaos.

Chaos: Are you here yet ?

JuiceBagger: Is he still here, because I just got here I'm outside now.

Chaos: Yeah he is still here. Last time I checked he was still upstairs. I got the picture of him just like you asked.

JuiceBagger: Send it to me.

Chaos: Already done.

JuiceBagger waited for a couple moments as the picture came to his phone. As soon as he saw the picture of J

Gunna, he was overcome with the same emotions he had felt on the night of the crime.

He instantly felt emotions to kill and destroy everything in its path in order to get to this maggot of a man.

However, also in the picture he saw Chaos smiling as if he was talking a selfie.

JuiceBagger texted Chaos immediately.

JuiceBagger: I thought I told you to not let him see you ? How did you get him to take this picture with you?

Chaos: I did what you asked me to didn't I ? As long as the means make the result.

JuiceBagger: LOL you did do that and FYI it's * As long as the end results justify the means!

Chaos: LOL yeah my sister used to say that all the time before she went missing.

JuiceBagger: Missing ? I want to know more about it later. But you still didn't answer me on how you got a picture with him ?

Chaos: Some people just want to be famous even if it's hood famous.

JuiceBagger: That is so very true. I will text you later. Go in your room and help me keep a look out for the police. Do you have those binoculars I gave you?

Chaos: Yes.

JuiceBagger: Okay I'll let you know when everything is over. What apartment does he live in again just for confirmation?

Chaos: 727.

JuiceBagger: Okay let me know if anything is up.

Chaos: He always takes the stairs!!!

JuiceBagger smiled as he thought to himself that Chaos could prove to be a soldier in the making. Even though he didn't want to look at it like that, he was proud of the child and his striking capabilities, as well as his ability to have exceptional observational skills.

Skills were needed in this life and he could use a few pointers from the youngster once this was over.

It truly showed that you were never too old to be able to learn from anyone. The ones who thought that, were the ones who ended up in the graveyard with flowers streaming over their caskets.

JuiceBagger entered the building with his backpack in tow. Careful not to spill the contents inside because it wouldn't be pretty for himself, or anyone else, who wasn't the designated recipient of what he had to dish out.

He had took to great lengths to change his appearance. Instead of having his beard and goatee, he was clean-shaven. Instead of having on his customary Urban Wear which consisted of jeans, Timberlands, and a white icy t-shirt, he was dressed in a casual suit with a tie that would make Steve Harvey slap his fashion designer !

Instead of the bling and ice that he had no problem flaunting and wearing, he chose to wear some plain black rosary beads. He had even cut off his beloved dreads and replaced it with a bald head. A Mr. Clean, as his grandmother called it. He had shined his head so good, that Steve Harvey would slap himself this time !

For the extra layer of security he had purchased some flowers from the flower shop so it would give a false sense of calm to the situation when it first happened.

J Gunna was known to tote heavy machinery and JuiceBagger knew that he had to be delicate. This was why he wore a new tactical vest, and this time he chose to pack twin Berettas. Police issue.

Come to think of it these two guns belonged to a police officer who was no longer amongst the living, due to his greedy ways.

So in that regard, JuiceBagger knew that he was safe from any type of prosecution in case he had to dump the weapons in the process of getting away from the scene.

JuiceBagger entered the building with no problems whatsoever, and he immediately took the stairs and posted up in the stairwell on the 6th floor, Giving him enough time to wait however long he had to wait. He could go up or down the stairs depending on the situation. He wanted this to go as planned because he had dreamed of this on many many nights.

JuiceBagger looked at his Casio watch and saw that it was going on 7:30 p.m. He had been in the stairwell for over a hour. Even though it was a long time, he had no problem with waiting a million years, for a chance to squash this cockroach and make him wish that he never was born.

He knew that by the standards of observation pointed out by Chaos, J Gunna always left his apartment at 7:45 every night, just around the time that the streets got dark, and the sun was kicking off his shoes and letting the moon take the night shift.

At 7:45 on the head, he heard commotion in the stairwell about two floors up and automatically assumed it was his target and he got up from where he was seated after taking a few moments to gather his thoughts.

He didn't have to guess who it was because whoever it was, was so involved a conversation that they didn't have a care in the world about anything else going on around them.

This made JuiceBagger smile with a smile that would put Any Smiling Emoji to shame. He thought to himself, "Maybe just maybe, this would be easier than he imagined."

As the person came down the stairs at a casual pace JuiceBagger began to get the case of jittery nerves as he always did when he was going to fuck up someone's life.

But with this being more personal than ever, he had decided not to indulge in smoking the recreational marijuana that soothed his nerves.

"Tell that bitch ass motherfucka that J Gunna is about to come through and get that money, and let it be known if he is short by a dollar or a nickel, Im going to cut him a new face with this razor blade I just bought. Tell that nigga I said play with me if he wants to, it'll be his ass that he packs for lunch for his punk-ass kid."

JuiceBagger now knew that it was indeed the person that he had come to see about, who was walking down the stairs towards his demise.

JuiceBagger continued to walk up the stairs as he found out from the horse's mouth himself that this was indeed who he was here to pay a visit.

He really didn't know how he was going to go about carrying out this mission, but he knew that he was good at thinking on the fly.

As soon as J Gunna was within range of him and he was sure that J Gunna could see him below, he intentionally stumbled on a stair and dropped the bouquet of flowers on the stairs directly in the path of J Gunna so as to block off any type of stepping around the flowers.

Even though he knew J Gunna wasn't worth a gram of salt, he didn't think that he would be a total asshole to just disregard a person in clear distress. As fate would have it, his assumptions were true because as soon as J Gunna saw him he said,

"Oh shit blood, you good bro? Ay swizzy I'ma hit you back and don't go around blowing that money we just came up on, tricking on no bitch."

JuiceBagger thought to himself, "this nigga is so fucking lame. He just don't know what he got coming."

After listening intently for a second, J Gunna said, "Okay Blood, get at me in a few. One Love." JuiceBagger had to control his emotions for a few more pivotal seconds, so as not to blow his cover as he looked at J Gunna through the spectacles that cover his face.

He could see in J Gunna's eyes that he had the potential for violence at any giving moment. Her knew he had to play his role like Denzel Washington or else he wouldn't keep the element of surprise, and potentially fuck up this whole situation.

In response to J Gunna's question, JuiceBagger said "Yeah I'm okay man. I'm just having a long day. I thought that these flowers would cheer my grandmother up. She just came home from attending my uncle's funeral so her spirits are not up to par right now.".

J Gunna took a look at him sizing him up and not seeing anything in his demeanor to suggest anything amidst, he gave him the benefit of the doubt as he let go of the pistol that he was clutching.

He himself had a grandmother and he knew what it was like to go through situations like this. He just wanted to help pick up the flowers scattered in the stairwell so he could be on his way.

JuiceBagger also noticed the subtile movement in the way that J Gunna let go of his waistband, so he knew exactly where the pistol was located at.

His goal was to make him turn around so that he could get the drop on him. That would make it easier to handle him without any type of drama that woukd cause gunfire in the stairwell.

After contemplating several ideas in about 30 seconds JuiceBagger decided to play the clumsy role. As he bent down to grab a flower from the top step, he allowed his foot to slip as he fell forward and grabbed onto the railing to catch his balance.

As this was happening, his glasses he intentionally wore flew off his face and landed a couple feet behind J Gunna as JuiceBagger yelled out in frustration.

"Fuck, I can't get nothing right I'm too damn clumsy for my own good."

JuiceBagger went to reach for them, but knowing the instincts of the street he knew that J Gunna probably wouldn't want him to be behind him, especially not knowing who this individual was.

That was how people got shot in the back of the head. Not knowing it was coming. And just as he assumed, J Gunna stopped him and said," I got this Blood, seems like you are having a long day for real. Let me help you out and get those for you." JuiceBagger inwardly smiled to himself and in his mind he said,"Like clockwork".

He allowed J gunna to turn his back and make himself a target for a surprise when he turned back around. JuiceBagger pulled out both the Berettas from behind his waist as he waited for J Gunna to turn around.

He had the drop on his prey and he wasn't about to let his let this big mouth bass get off the hook. There was no way in hell.

As J Gunna turned around to pass JuiceBagger his glasses he nearly shit his pants when he saw himself staring down the barrel of two pearl-handled Berettas.

He immediately threw his hands up and tried to plead for his life." Please don't kill me blood. I got money, powder, jewelry, whatever you want but please don't take my soul from me."

JuiceBagger looked at him dead in his eyes and told him," I'm not here to talk to you, so let's handle this like men and let me get what you got so I can be on my way. Let's go upstairs to 727 and let me get me. If you try anything stupid or try to make a scene, I'll make one for you. I'll make a crime scene with you in the starring role !"

J Gunna looked deeply into JuiceBaggers eyes and saw something that he did not notice before. He saw a man on a mission and someone who would not stop until he got what he came for or he left a trail of blood in the process.

It was at that moment that J Gunna decided that he wasn't going to buck. At least not yet. Not while the gun was pointed at him and he was in the line of fire, like a victim standing in the middle of a firing squad.

He would wait until he had him in his crib before he had made a move.

He was interrupted by JuiceBagger telling him, "Don't think about what you thinking about, cuz I will open your head up just to see what the fuck you was thinking about. Don't try and be no damn hero to save your soul, just go with the flow like a hot 16, and we'll see if you got enough talent to get signed to live alot records. Please don't think I won't let these guns make a new instrumental. Now let's go pussy !"

JuiceBagger was careful to stay within arms reach as he left the flowers in the stairwell. He had to make his move effectively and efficiently as possible, so he would have minimum collateral damage in case a motherfuker wanted to save this nigga.

They made it to J Gunna's apartment which happened to be at the very end of the hallway closest to the stairs. JuiceBagger looked around and saw that the coast was clear as a brand new pair of goggles.

Free of anything or anyone who would be in the position to do anything or say anything. In order words, anyone who could be a potential witness to him being there.

JuiceBagger grabbed J Gunna close by the neck and told him ,"Don't die in this spot because I will drop you and let you stay where you lay. Now ease the keys out of your pocket and open the door. I'm not here to hurt you but I will."

JuiceBagger wanted to give him a sense of thinking that nothing would happen to him so he could gain entry to the apartment, because if he decided to buck in the hallway then it wouldn't be good for the whole situation and it would complicate things.

He felt the tension disappear from J Gunna as you he retrieved the keys from his pocket and put them in the door.

"Hurry up nigga." JuiceBagger told him before continuing, "If anybody comes out here before we get inside I'm going to kill your ass and them so move your ass if you want to live. I only want what I came for."

As J Gunna opened the door and pushed it open he was certainly hoping that this his dog has somehow managed to get out of the cage, because he needed more than a little bit of help.

As soon as JuiceBagger heard the door open up and he felt the door give way to space and opportunity, he shoved J Gunna in the house and gave him a double tap.

Some people would refer that as meaning two shots to the head, but in his mind that term was strictly reserved for cops to describe it that way. JuiceBagger gunbutted J Gunna as hard as he could with each gun to make sure he went down without a fight.

MAPPPPPP!!!! MAPPPPPP!!!!

And down he went!

J Gunna was thinking about his dog when suddenly he took notice of feeling pain in his head that resemble a bomb blowing in his head and he saw a twinkle of white lights before he was enveloped in darkness and he felt himself falling to the ground.

JuiceBagger wanted him to fall on his face but he knew that he couldn't let that happen due to the simple fact that he didn't want any type of noise to signal anybody below.

As well as the fact that he didn't want this mark ass buster to die from too much head trauma so he grabbed J Gunna as he was about to fall and stopped his impact with the ground from being a solid thud,to just being a small and inaudible thump.

He turned around and locked the door and got to business as his mind shifted to Killa mode. He wanted to bust a nut he was so happy and bloodthirsty.

He took off his backpack and got out the roll of extra duty duct tape and taped the fuck out of J Gunna. He used the entire roll taping his legs together and then his feet.

Then he checked his breathing, before using his own razor blade that fell out of his coat pocket to cut off J Gunnas shirt.

He wanted to make sure that his upper body was nude because he has special plans for Julian. He had found J Gunnas state ID and he almost pissed his pants at the sight of discovering his name to be Julian.

"Jesus Take the wheel", he said to himself as he use the rest of the tape to bind J Gunnas hands behind his back, and he made him a special strip for his mouth.

After doing that he remembered the flowers in the stairwell and he sent a text to Chaos telling him to get the flowers and give them to his mother.

After receiving the text back from Chaos to confirm that he had did as instructed, he told Chaos to keep a watch out for him and he would give him $5,000 as well as his mother $10,000. As usual, the response he got from Chaos was

Chaos: Okay! $$$$$$$$$

He smiled to himself as he knew he had found a new protege to take under his wing and make him happy and proud like a new father welcoming a baby boy in the world.

JuiceBagger went off in search of whatever he could find until sleepyhead awoke from his nap. He wanted to see if his home invasion skills were up to par as he timed herself for 10 minutes to see what he could find.

Before all of this, he put on a new pair of plastic gloves, because the last pair of gloves that he had on was sticky from all the tape he used on J Gunna.

He didn't want anything to connect him back to the scene, when it turned into a scene!!.

After tearing up the whole house from the inside out in less than 10 minutes, he was forced to conclude that this house was a front for just living and fucking bitches, due to the lack of care and home maintenance that any man should, and would, have in his house.

So, with all of the particulars out of the way, he went back into the living room and filled up a glass of cold water and filled ice cubes in it to give it a colder chill to it, and waited ten more minutes to see if the beauty and the beast would rise on his own.

After coming to the consensus that he would not wake up on his own, JuiceBagger walked over to him and slapped the P off of that box of potatoes!!!

POOOOOOWWWWWW!!!!!!!

If that didn't make Martha Stewart proud, he didn't know what would, as he dumped the whole glass of water on J Gunna's head and whispered in his ear,

"Wake yo dumb ass up hoe!!!"

J Gunna woke up feeling constricted of any movement and seeing JuiceBagger he instantly remembered what was going down at that very moment in time.

"Mmmmpppphhh!!!!!"

"Mpppppppppphhh!!!!!"

JuiceBagger look at him and said, "Shut the hell up until I ask you to talk. Believe me with God love, I'm going to give you a chance to talk. But first I want to make it clear to you, that at any given time if you do not comply with anything I ask you to do, then you will pay a price. The price may be small or it may be great. But I can guarantee you that you will pay a price. A healthy one. A price that may determine your health and survival. You think you are tough. I'm tougher. You think you are strong, I'm stronger. You think you are smart, I'm smarter. I'm your damn daddy, until I say otherwise. Nod your fucking if you understand me you piece of shit."

J Gunna had the look of a defeated man as he took his mind and soul to another place and forced himself to nod.

JuiceBagger began to pace back and forth as he continued," Okay, now with that out of the way, I want you to make a call to your boy swizzy for me and tell him that you need him to come over. Don't ask me my, just ask me when. Seeing as though you can't ask me, I'll tell you. I want him to come over here right now so all three of us can have a discussion about who is the master of all Masters. I need to figure out a few things and that won't be too hard once he gets here is that understood?"

Another nod confirmed that he understood and he was able to move to phase two of his plan.

JuiceBagger grabbed J Gunna's phone and peeled off the tape around his mouth. He had turned up the music system that he found by the television just in case J Gunna was a yeller.

In past home invasions he learned the difference between a yeller and a mime. A yeller would yell at the first opportunity they got, while a mime would remain silent and go with the program in hopes of living to see another day.

J Gunna was a mime. He would comply with everything he was asked to do so that he would not lose his soul in the process.

JuiceBagger liked that fact and he gave specific instructions on what to say and when to get off the phone. Anything construed as a prearranged signal would result in another gun butt to the cranium and J Gunna knew he could not sustain one more of those.

JuiceBagger dialed the number and turned the music down just enough to hear the phone as he placed it on speaker.

RRRRIIIINNNGGGG.....please enjoy this Verizon ringback tone while your party is being reached.

" Many men wish death upon me blood in my eyes dog and I can't see.. I'm just trying....

He heard swizzy answer in the background..

"What's good bro?"

JuiceBagger could hear Swizzy in the background moving about wherever he was at.

He held the barrel of the gun to J Gunna's head as he replied," Shiiiiiddddd,bI was leaving the building when those bitties Shaniqua and Mookie stopped me bro. Them hoes in the bathroom getting freshened up right now blood I need you to get your ass over here and help me give these bitches a run for their money blood!!"

Swizzy smiled to himself as he said,"Damn bro, I was comfortable counting this money up but I'm bout to come through that muhfucka like a tsunami and lay body parts everywhere. Hahahaha.

J Gunna faked a laugh and told him," You brazy blood just get here before these biddies run me in a hole somewhere bro."

" Bet it up."

" Bet it up."

JuiceBagger grabbed the phone and hung up the phone as he slapped the tape back on J Gunna's mouth.

He was excited that he would be able to extract revenge from both of the individuals who did him dirty. It was better that he got them together because he didn't like chasing anybody for any reason. Especially not to kill them. This was good. Real good. He got out his personal phone and began to text Chaos.

JuiceBagger: Do you know what swizzy looks like?

Chaos: Yes, I know what he looks like.

JuiceBagger: Okay Im expecting him, but I don't want him to come up without me knowing.

Chaos: Okay I'll let you know when I see him, and what he is wearing.

JuiceBagger: Okay. Just let me know ASAP.

He went back and sat down on the couch to clear his mind for a few minutes, before he opened up his backpack to check on something, and to retrieve the stun gun taser that he had brought for this occasion. He would not mess this up because both of these individuals would pay for what they had done to him, with their lives! He would make sure of it!!!!!

Chapter Ten

Juice stood outside of J Gunna's apartment waiting on word to come back from Chaos on what to do and what this dude had on.

He wanted to make sure that this was the right person because he had some devious shit up his sleeve that he didn't want to impose on an innocent person

He wasn't worried about J Gunna getting out of the house, because he had him tied up to the shower rail in the bathroom. He wasn't going anywhere for a while. So he could cry his heart out because he was in for a hell of a ride and he wasn't the driver.

It was times like this that made him feel like he was a true hypocrite. He didn't want to hurt nobody but at times it was just inevitable, in life to go through nothing but drama. Unless your skin color was a distinct pale white with a shade of red and pink.

He wasn't in no way, shape, or form, a racist. Not by any level or means. Most of his friends were white. From Andrew Jackson, To George Washington, to Alexander Hamilton,to Ulysses Grant,to Benjamin Franklin. He just understood that the way the land of the free, was so inhibited and influenced to favor those of different descent, so he had to get it by any means and this type of consequences became a thing of the normal happenstances in his line of work. He just prayed that his life would not be in vain. Because for all the bad that he did in his life he wanted to do so much more good in the hopes that the scales would at least be balanced on the day of judgment. If there was no heaven or hell, then so be it. But he felt that there should be a balance to the negative and positive deeds that a person did in their lifetime.

JuiceBagger went into the stairwell to light up a Newport 100 cigarette while he waited. He had to calm his nerves because that would be the only way he would make it through this experience. He wanted to just blast the gun and let the gun rip without any type of remorse or regard for anyone or anything.

That was the savage part of him talking though. He knew that there was way more important things to do in life, and he could not afford to mess anything up for him or his crew.

His loyalty was something that saved a lot of individuals from a certain death. But he was not to be the judge and jury for all the dumb individuals who crossed paths with him. ONLY those who crossed the line. He didn't look for trouble intentionally but if it came, then why not bust his gun. As his thoughts were swirling like a fish in a fishbowl, his cell phone vibrated signaling that he had a text message.

Chaos: Swizzy is here. He is wearing a New York Knicks jersey, blue jeans,and blue Foamposites. He is taking the stairs now.

JuiceBagger: Okay give me a minute.

Chaos: Okay.

JuiceBagger made his way down the stairs and stopped on the fifth floor again then decided that it would be better if he came from the upper floor this time so he wouldn't have to drag this muhfucka up the stairs.

His plan was to zap the fuck out of Swizzy with his stun gun as soon as he saw him. No other way around that. He he clicked the switch on the lock on J Gunna's door so that the door would stay unlocked until the lock release mechanism was taken off, or the door was locked from the inside. He hurriedly went to the fifth floor to wait for

Swizzy. He was packing only the stun gun and a knife at this moment. He knew that was risky but he didn't want to be carrying too many weapons. His hands and feet were licensed and registered with the police department, so he knew he could paralyze and brutalize the average muhfucka.

But he also knew he would only get one shot at making this shot with the taser count. It was a Taser Pulse with a laser and LED, capable of 10000 volts of power. If that wasn't enough to take this dude down to his knees then he didn't know what would.

As swizzy came into sight on the lower level of the staircase JuiceBagger knew that it would be no room or margin for error. He already had the beam locked on for sight. Now he had to pick the right moment to aim and fire.

But just like J Gunna, Swizzy was so consumed in his phone conversation that he was totally unaware of the dangers that presented themselves around him. And unfortunately for him, he was about to be a full of misfortune for not being careful.

JuiceBagger didn't even have to rush to pull the trigger because Swizzy had stopped in front of the door to the stairwell to continue his conversation with whoever was on the other end of the phone.

"Yeah baby, just make sure you have daddy a good cooked meal when I get back from putting in work with Gunna."

JuiceBagger had heard enough and was about to pull the trigger when someone from the 8th floor attempted to open the stairwell.

JuiceBagger pointed the beam at a young boy and tried to shoo him away with his hand, but the boy continue to stand there in shock until JuiceBagger pulled out his whole knot and gave it to him.

He didn't have time to pull off a 20 or 10 because he was on a mission. But after getting the money the young child speed away and allowed the door to slam.

BOOOOOOOM!!!!

"Shit!"

JuiceBagger cursed under his breath as he was forced to go into full combat mode. He jumped down the flight of stairs and kicked Swizzy in the shin and brought the butt of the taser across the bridge of Swizzy's nose with such a force that, even mother nature would pay homage.

Even though it wasn't a gun it was enough force and enough objective weight, that the taser served it's purpose and fucked his world up.

"Ahhhhhhgrhrhhh".

Swizzy was screaming in pain until JuiceBagger silenced him with the steady tapping of voltage to his nuts that would incense a grizzly bear !

It was no wasted effort involved because Swizzy dropped to the floor and started foaming out of the mouth.

JuiceBagger quickly put the taser in his waist not bothering to take the prongs out of Swizzy.

He didn't think that he could anyway, because the prongs were stuck in the fabric of his jeans and would only come out with effort and time. Something that JuiceBagger didn't have at the present moment.

He quickly moved Swizzy from in front of the door and checked the coast to make sure that he didn't have to fuck nobody else up, because his tolerance for any type of interruptions was up to his neck like a turtleneck.

Seeing nobody in the way, JuiceBagger quickly grabbed him and drug him to the apartment. Once there he opened it up and pulled him aside and locked the door and put on the safety chain as well. He was going to make sure nobody left this little shop of horrors!

The small effort had left him winded like a bagpipe player ,but he couldn't rest until this muhfucka with restrained.

Instead of even pulling out the tape, he resorted to pulling out zip ties to use on Swizzy.

This was so that he could strip swizzy butt booty ass naked. Not on no gay shit, but because he had special plans of torture for both of these muhfuckas.

He put Swizzy into the bathroom with J Gunna. Finding a new sense of strength he decided to walk over to J Gunna and give him a sample of Ms Taser Jackson too. He placed the taser on J Gunna's nuts and pulled the trigger.

" Tat tat tat tat tat tat tat tat tat tat"

All of a sudden, J Gunna began to shake and seize as if he was twerking, and shaking nothing but ass. JuiceBagger laughed out loud to himself as he had to remove the tape from J Gunna's mouth so that he could let out some foam too.

"Damn", he thought to himself, "This taser make motherfukers foam up out the mouth like wax on the floor before it settles. That shit is going to kill a muhfucka." Then he looked at the taser and saw that the level of intensity was on maximum power. He thought that was funny as he started to crack up in laughter and said," My apologies guys, I didn't mean to give y'all the max."

Just then he saw Swizzy going into convulsions and raced over to him and began to feel for a pulse, and found it beginning to get real shallow.

"Shit!!! Y'all bitches making my dick hard as a motherfuckin E.R. doctor but I'm not about to let y'all die on me because I'm not done with y'all yet. Now man the fuck up !"

Seeing no response, he began to give Swizzy mouth to mouth and chest compressions to open his breathing channel, so he could get oxygen in his lungs to withstand the loss of whatever air that the foaming out the mouth caused him to lose. While he was working on Swizzy, he looked back over at J Gunna and focused his attention to see if he would start having convulsions as well but he was surprised to see that J Gunna was taking this like a true fighter. A true champion.

"I'm proud of you J. You took that well.." he said as he laughed and furiously fought to revive swizzy and bring him back to consciousness.

It was a tedious task, but he did it with the grace of a higher power. Swizzy came back to life conscious enough for JuiceBagger to slap the shit out of him for trying to take the easy way out.

SMAAAAAAACCCKKK!!!!!

"Bitch you better not die until I tell you that you can die on me. This is not a game and you will not play me like a PlayStation 5, Xbox one Nintendo Wii or whatever else game there is to play. I will tell you just like I told Sunshine here, if you try and fuck up my groove, then you will dance to a beat so motherfuckin funky that Michael Jackson will have to come up with a new track from the grave. Now if you honestly think I am the one, then try me. You will not survive this experience either way, but I will let you choose the gracious way out or the rebellious way out. Both ways include me doing some pretty fucked up up shit to you, but you deserve every ounce of creativity that I mustered up for this occasion. I know I'm talking a lot but I'm pretty sure that you both would rather me talking, than to do what I planned for you right now. So allow me to tell you why I am doing what I am doing, and at the end of this you will...."

"HELLLLLLLPPPPPPP, HEEELLLLLPPPPP, HEEEEELLLLLLLLLPPPPPPP."

J Gunna began to scream at the top of his lungs until JuiceBagger silenced him with a vicious right hand to the temple. That was a hit that was designed to take the fight out of any individual and one that JuiceBagger had used on so many people in the Police Athletic League.

They had banned JuiceBagger from boxing any boys his age, and he was most seldomly forced to get his ass kicked by the older boys in the boxing program, until they could no longer control him or his speed or his offense or his defense.

JuiceBagger was mad that he had to use his hands and he hit J Gunna with another right to the section of his ribs where it would cave in a couple ribs.

He didn't want to hit him in the solar plexus, because he was already unconscious. He didn't want to kill him due to the deprivation of oxygen. He ran out of the bathroom, to go and get his backpack that he had left on the couch in the living room.

Even though this was a small apartment, it was spacious enough for him to get to work and make sure that it was precise and fell in line with his personal standards of inflicting torment and pain.

When it came to that he held himself in high regards and he wanted to always perform to the best of his ability. That was the way he was. Groomed by the streets to be the best at whatever you set yourself and your mind to.

After retrieving the backpack he went back into the bathroom and decided that it wasn't enough room in the bathroom for what he wanted to do. He thought about taking both of them into separate rooms and making them suffer for one at a time but decided against it.

What better way than to allow them the dignity to die together. After all, nobody on this Earth wanted to die alone. There was plenty of nights when he thought about his older brother who died alone in a bathroom. His older brother William died from a sugar induced coma. He had been unfortunate to have diabetes and he didn't know that he had diabetes. He died from eating sweets like a normal kid, and not knowing that he was killing himself slowly. He didn't have time to react when his heart just gave out on him. So in that regard JuiceBagger was going to let them at least feel some comfort in knowing that they would die together.

He grabbed a smelling salt and snapped the pack in half to activate the smelling chemicals that released the vapors that packed a punch that would make Floyd Mayweather say" Jesus Take the wheel !"

JuiceBagger placed it under J Gunna's nose and it instantly woke him up from wherever he was at temporarily. It must have rattled his senses so much, that J Gunna just looked into the space past JuiceBaggern, noteven recognizing him standing in front of him.

JuiceBagger shook his head and held the smell salt in front of his nose until he was sure that he had come to his senses and had regained true composure on what the hell was going on.

It was evident from the look on his face that he didn't know what this was all about and JuiceBagger loved it like that.

He would find out soon enough that you don't fuck with someone who has the insanity level that Jack the Ripper, The Son of Sam, Pablo Escobar and Adolf Hitler would envy. A son of a bitch with more screws missing than a empty toolbox. It just ain't there muhfucka.

JuiceBagger looked at his watch and saw that it was after 9 p.m. and he had to do some things later that night. He couldn't miss the meeting with Nouchy. But he would just have to be a couple hours late. Shitttttt, better late than never.

Nouchy would talk shit but he would understand without words what time it was, and would wait till the right moment to curse him out and give him admonishment for the blatant disrespect at the level of rank within the organization.

JuiceBagger moved both men into the hallway and began to set up his shop of horrors. He would have to keep it strictly how he had planned to keep it. No bloody crime scene that would get a motherfucker messed up in the process. He didn't want his"Cleaners" having to clean up alot of blood. He felt strongly about looking out for the well-being of others. Like his grandma used to tell him,"It's more than one way to skin a cat".

He picked up his phone and sent a text to his Chaos.

JuiceBagger: I'm going to need you to take some clothes to the cleaners for me in a few so be on standby.

He didn't wait for a response because it was honestly no telling what the Chaos was doing right now and he wanted to make sure that he didn't waste too much time worrying about what the couldn't control right now.

Seeing that both J Gunna and Swizzy had no clue what the hell was going on right now, he decided to clue them in so it wouldn't make them scratch their heads too much longer. And he wanted to give them the reason why they would not be breathing in about 5 hours from now.

Walking back and forth down the hallway he began to speak but thought about something and walk over to J Gunna and stood on his balls as he told him, "I left that tape off your mouth on purpose so you would try me again that way I could take out my screwdriver, and take your eye out of the socket with it like plucking a chicken. Please don't make me make you a believer, because only God knows what you will be after I'm done with you. Do I make myself clear ? Or do I have to cut one of your balls off?"

He watched J Gunna nod and squeal in confirmation. He walk over to Swizzy and told him I would cover your mouth but you are a good captive, you haven't given me any reason to knock you out or fuck you up so let's keep it that way okay?"

With a nod of confirmation that he understood JuiceBagger continued to speak.

" I really don't want you to think that I am picking on the two of you for no apparent reason so I'm going to show you a picture and I want you to tell me do you recognize this person."

He pulled out his phone and pulled up a recent photo of him in the club before he changed his appearance and showed it to them. As they recognized who it was in the picture they both play their cases at the same time.

"Man we are sorry ....I'm sorry man... Whoever that is to you tell him it wasn't personal ....It was...."

JuiceBagger held up his hands and told them both," Be quiet and just shut the fuck up . I don't want to hear nothing. This perfect person happens to be........ ME!!!!!!! Haha.... I'm in the flesh. Do you recognize me without all my hair? Matter fact don't say nothing, because this is not a situation where I'm trying to connect with friends for old times sake. I just want to know where my shit at so I can get what's mines and kill you and be out of here. So who wants to talk first ? "

Neither of them said nothing as they realized that this was a situation they could not talk themselves out of. The realization that death was permanent had set them and their ways of stubbornness.

If they were going to die anyway, then it was only right that they would go to their graves as gangsters. True legends didn't give up a ounce of information, no matter what type of situation they found themselves in. It didn't matter anymore. So it was to God be the glory, and the streets be the fame. The flames of hell would be waiting to engulf them anyway for the deeds of their past. JuiceBagger recognized it for what it was and he couldn't even be mad at them, because in a peculiar similar situation, he wouldn't spill the beans and he would endure whatever he had to in order to ensure that his family was safe in all definitions of the word.

He grabbed the roll of duct tape and began to pull off strips for their mouth.

At this time both of them began to yell with a ferociousness of a wounded baby cub in hopes that the lioness or lion would come to their rescue. This only earned them a vicious kick to the head to silence them both, as he kick both of them unconscious.

Some muhfuckas just had to learn the hard way about his ability to deliver kicks and blows to the right spot to make a bitch tap out or get knocked out. And at this very moment and time JuiceBagger didn't give two shits or a rat's ass about these two scumbags.

After taping their mouth shut and checking the restraints on them both, he felt comfortable enough to wake them back up with the smelling salts and bring them to their senses.

" Hellooooooooo sleepy heads, are we ready to get this over with because I admit this is starting to get boring. My hands and feet are more valuable than having to use them to knock y'all out momentarily. So I'm about to knock you out permanently. You shouldn't have robbed me for what was mines. I put a lot of thought into what I would do when I found you goofballs and I came up with the perfect solution to my problems. So here goes nothing.

He looked in both of their eyes and saw nothing but fear. He continued speaking,

"Before I do what I am going to do, I want to tell you a little story about my life just to give y'all a picture of where this idea came from. You know nature is a beautiful thing. I love everything about it because it has order in it. Things have to happen in order for other things to happen to create all types of things. Let's take tornadoes for example. What causes tornadoes? Anybody want to answer?"

After seeing that neither of them knew or even cared he continued on his rant feeling like Kanye West while he was giving through his nervous breakdown.

" I'll give you the short version. A tornado is the result of updrafts and downdrafts in a thunderstorm caused by unstable air interacting with the wind shear resulting in a tilting of the wind shear to form an upright tornado vortex. Anyways, I don't want to hold y'all up cuz I know y'all have some place to go. But I'll tell you that growing up as a child I was always mesmerized by animals. I love all kinds of animals, simply because their breed is different from the breed of humans. They only kill to survive, while humans kill just for the fun of it or to gain something that essentially they may not need to survive. Take you two for instance. Robbing me because you wanted what I had. Not because you needed it. You simply wanted it and in the process of acquiring it, you didn't care about my discomfort.

"You didn't care whether I had a family who counts on me to support them, and take care of them, so that they won't have to rob, or steal,or kill, or cheat or envy be a typical shithead like you two. Some people work for a living. No matter what they do to get the funds, or means to provide. Which brings me back to my story about my love of animals. My mom used to take me to the zoo. I saw every animal imaginable but out of all animals I fell in love with the insects. So every trip to the zoo, I would run right to the insect section. It got so crazy that my mother had to take me to the doctor because she felt that it was becoming a problem. I only wanted insect books and books that defined my love for what I loved.

In my teen years I found out that meanings of people who love what I love and what the terms were for people like me. I found out that I had a "Philia" which means I have a fondness or abnormal love for a specific specified thing.

Which brings me to my special present for you Mr Swizzy."

With that being said you JuiceBagger went to his makeshift shop that he had set up and he pulled out a black seal proof case that contained 1 species of his most prized insect.

He figured that since he was in the business of doing things the very best, why not start off with the best of the best.

He also picked up two plastic spoons and a jar of honey that he had brought along for the occasion. This would be the first time that he had ever done something like this, but he knew the end result would be fatal, and it would take hours to accomplish the deed. He didn't mind the wait. That is what made this all the more worth it.

His mind was perverted and sick and twisted like an arubics cube but it was all to the good in order to prove a point. A point that he was not to be fucked with all together.

JuiceBagger grabbed the spoon and placed it in the jar of honey and sprinkled a little of it all over Swizzy from his head to his toes. Even on his dick and balls. He made sure he lathered it up just right so that the honey wouldn't be too thick for his homies to do what they did.

After that was done, he took the seal proof box and opened it and took a spoonful of his homies and sprinkled them all over Swizzy's private areas

first, as he looked down on him and spoke softly "This is for my myremecophilia (Love of ants) These are called Fire Ants. But these are not just any Fire Ant. These are Brazilian fire ants known for their extremely painful bites. Right now you are in terrible pain as you should be and I could care less."

Swizzy lay on the floor thinking to himself as his body was overcome with such pain that he didn't know what was happening. He just knew that he should have never fucked with this evil bastard standing in front of him. He wished that he didn't do so many of the crazy things that he did in his lifetime but it was too late to cry and ask God for forgiveness, so he would just take his lumps and bruises like a man and it would be what it would be not that he cared about dying. He just wanted to see his son one more time. His son was only nine years old and he wouldn't get to hold him and feel his arms around him or his embrace.

All because of the decision to rob this punk ass motherfucker standing here with a grin that would make Satan proud.

He was okay with the fact he would die, but oh shit, did a fire ant just crawl up inside his dick ? Oh my God. This ant was biting the inside of his pee hole. He tried to wiggle, but the bonds were too tight, he said a prayer to whoever it was that it was stopped but this ant was having his way in that motherfucker. Damn!!!! he thought to himself. I gotta piss on myself to get this muhfucka up out of here, or he going to cause me hell on Earth

before I even go meet the devil. With that, he told his mind to will himself to pee but he thought about it he hadn't drunk any fluids in over three hours. Added to the fact that he had used the bathroom before he came because he didn't want to start fucking and not be able to bust a nut because he had to piss.

Shit!!!! he couldn't piss, so maybe some precum would get this ant out. He started to visualize all the pornos in his lifetime that he watched, in hopes he could find a solution to this madness. God help me he pleaded.

JuiceBagger walked over to J Gunna with a bigger case and the jar of honey. Instead of lathering him up, he just poured the whole thing over him and covered him in honey. He opened the case and dump the contents on top of him with a tenacious look on his face.

JuiceBagger spoke to him and told him"This is for my Arachnephilia. These right here are Brazilian Wandering Spiders. They are capable of injecting a powerful neurotoxin which is more deadlier than a black widow's bite times twenty. So these critters will eat on this honey until they get tired of it and want a different substance and choose to bite you instead.

By biting you, you will be shot with toxins that will shut down your neurological systems one by one all of your organs will be reduced to putty. Silly putty for a silly ass nigga. What you think ?"

J Gunna was overcome with emotions as he could already feel a couple bites from the spiders there was six spiders on him and he no longer wanted to be brave. He wanted to cry like a bitch and make his mama comfort him.

The pain was bad and intense and he didn't want to take it anymore so he tried to hold his breath to commit suicide but that wouldn't work in any way without something constricting his air.

Wait! What was that ? Oh God! Please no!!! It was as if one of the spiders had read his mind because it was crawling up his stomach and ignoring the honey and it was looking for a way to do whatever it was thinking.

Just then, JuiceBagger saw what the spider wanted to do, so he took his knife and cut a hole in the mouth part of the tape on J Gunna's face and sat back to watch.

He then decided to dump the rest of the colony of fire ants on Swizzy's face and watch the outcome of that as well.

One thing for sure, two things for certain he like this type of shit. This made him feel indebted to nature and he was in awe of it.

J Gunna watched in horror as a spider began to hit his lip with his venom from his teeth and he began to notice his lip getting numb and he could no longer keep his mouth closed.

JuiceBagger watched in amazement as the spider pried open J Gunna's mouth and began to crawl down inside his mouth.

" Holy shit" he exclaimed,"Damn, that's a smart ass spider !" as he look at J Gunna and he could see on the mans face that he was being choked to death by a spider. His legs to wiggle as he screamed in fear knowing his death was fastly approaching. As the shaking stopped and the light faded from his eyes, JuiceBagger turned to Swizzy and saw that he had already died from the colony of ants that chewed a hole in his windpipe and was now bored and all over the place.

Since he missed the show he had to carry out the mission of killing all the creatures.

Noooooo.... He wouldn't do the spiders like that. He could use them again. But the ants wouldn't willingly climb back into the jar he had them in so he pulled out his insect spray and let the fire ants stay where they lay.

It was sad to kill them but he had shit to do. After getting the spiders minus the one still in J Gunna's throat, he packed all his stuff and exited the building into the familiar darkness of the night. Knowing that the world was less two savages........

Chapter Eleven

Over the next couple of days P Nouchy was out and about moving to and fro in an attempt to get things right for his mother's funeral. Even though he was filled with multiple emotions and transfixed upon doing what his mind was telling him to do, he knew that it was a time and place for everything.

A time to confront people and a time to be passive. If there was anything that he had learned from Jafar, it was that you had to have balance. You had to be able to separate the attachment and/or the application of 'feelings' in order to do what the present moment called for.

So as of right now the present moment called for him to get things done on the homefront before he could attend to matters in the street. Two things that he felt he needed to do, would require his undivided attention, which he couldn't properly give to the task at this time. " Better safe than sorry", he said to himself.

As a precaution he now carried with him a Glock 43 for his personal protection. His contact in the UK had reached out to him when the Glock 43 became available. The Glock 43 was a single stack 9mm pistol. Its size allowed for it to be ultra concealable and accurate.

With a built-in grip, built in beaver tail design, it allowed Nouchy to have a high and tight grip. The aggressive texture of the group let Nouchy operate and handle the gun more easily. The normal magazine size allowed for only six rounds to be in a ejected from the gun. Although that wasn't a bunch of rounds, Nouchy was qualified to take nothing but lethal shots at whoever targeted him. It wasn't as if he was expecting any kind of danger in any regard. He was more than capable of handling himself. He was only worried about taking care of everything that he had to do to ensure that his mother had a great and blessed home going service.

After all it was the least that he could do. His mother had been the type of person who was committed to making sure he had the best of everything growing up. Not just him. But his siblings and anyone else who came in contact with her. His mother had a spirit unlike any other and it was a devastating blow to see the matriarch of the family soon to be laid to rest. Just the mere thought of having to cope without her was something that he knew he would have to be strong in order to undertake such a task.

He could not let his grief about the situation impact him in such a way that it would be detrimental for his agendas. He needed to stay sharp and crisp at all times.

His first stop would be to the funeral home to check on the arrangements that he had briefly discussed with the funeral director.

He wanted his mother to be laid to rest in a satin Cherry solid hardwood casket with attached handles for the side of it.

Something that looked nice but was not over the top. He didn't want the uninvited or unwanted attention of anyone who may end up coming to his mother's funeral.

He wanted to give his mother an all gold 24-carat casket, but he thought better of it. He could already hear the admonishment from his mother.

"Boy, you better not put me in that attention seeker You know better than that. Now, I do want to look good for my last night out make sure you can get me something real nice. One of my favorite dresses will do just fine."

He smiled to himself because he really thought that he could do her home going service justice. He wanted to give her everything that she wanted in life and in death.

She wasn't picky by any means. She lived a simple life. Why should it be any different in this matter.

The meeting with the funeral director lasted 1 hour and 15 minutes. They discussed everything from the venue, to the size of the gathering before and after the service.

Even down to the route in which the hearse would travel to his mother's final resting place.

After ensuring himself over and over again that everything was down to a T, he decided to go over to the bank and speak to the banker about making the transfer of funds to the funeral home for the cover of costs.

He didn't want there to be any issues with anything concerning this situation. He didn't know if his brother would show up to the homegoing service for his mother. He would not stop him from attempting to come to the service, it would give him a chance to look into his brother's eyes as he asked him questions as to what happened that night.

Little did K Rouga know, the nurse on shift that night had told him all about the amount of time that his brother had spent in the room with his mother on the night of her death it was something that wasn't adding up.

There was a bond between his mother and K Rouga but to be real about the situation it wasn't nothing special. K Rouga was capable of having feelings for someone and then turn cold and icy towards them so it was something to be said about what was going on.

He knew how to play it. It wasn't going to be hard to find out what was going on. He had no issues with retrieving the information. It was more so of what he would do if the information he found out connected the dots in his gut feeling.

He would cross that bridge when it got to that point. But for now, he had to play it cool and make sure he was available for his family on what would be one of the hardest days of their lives.

Even though he was referred to as the "baby boy" in the family, he was the one who held the glue together. This was something that would be very challenging for his family but he would be right there to help them get through the tough time. Upon entering the bank he was met by the family bank manager who escorted him into the back office so that they could conduct business. He was caught up in his own thoughts to the extent that the manager had to call his name multiple times.

Nouchy!! Nouchy!! Nouchy!! The bank manager exclaimed before settling in his chair behind his lavish mahogany desk. He look down his nose through his Cartier glass to check that the man who had come to see him was paying attention. Even though this was a somber moment, the business that was to be conducted went by without a hitch. It actually went by in a blur so much so that Noichy didn't really recall much of the conversation up until the clerk said to the manager "Do you want to show Nouchy his mother's safety deposit box ?"

As soon as that was said Nouchy snap back to the present moment, promising the memories that he would be back to reengage with them the next chance he got.

He was taken aback and at a loss for words because he had been to this bank with his mother plenty of times, and they had never been to see any type of safety deposit box.

"Are you sure that my mother had a safety deposit box?" he asked the clerk who just so happened to look like a young Farrah Fawcett.

The clerk smiled at him and told him in a polite voice," It is a policy of this bank to know everything there is to know about the customers who entrust us with their savings, personal items,and anything else that the bank can store. Your mother has had this deposit box for 15 years. She always knew this day would come. Would you like us to show you the box ?"

Nouchy was still caught up in a trance as he just nodded his head and was led down the hallway toward the safety deposit box. He had never known what would possess his mother to have a deposit box but here he was being led to the safety-deposit room.

Inside the room was a mailbox row of boxes with multiple numbers embossed on them. It was a vast amount of boxes around a table that was nailed to the floor.

After looking at all the boxes in the room and checking the security cameras at the top of the ceiling, Nouchy stood directly in front of the open deposit box and stood there for what seemed like forever.

He heard the clerk say," I'll be right outside the door when you are done you can let me know when you are done".

After a silent approval from him she exited the room to leave him in peace. As he stood in front of the deposit box he could feel the presence of his mother he could smell the scent of the Este Lauder perfume that his mother wore.

He could feel the warmth of her breath on his neck bringing back memories that he knew he couldn't get rid of.

As he peered in the safe-deposit box he couldn't see anything inside of the safety deposit box except for a single white envelope.

He smiled to himself because once again, it was his mother's way of telling him that she was a simple woman. No extravagant jewelry, money piles, or family heirlooms were in chest in the deposit box. Nothing except for a measly letter that he was eager to read.

As he looked in at the envelope he could hear his mother's voice whispering to him, "Safeguard what's yours", over and over.

He heard her voice repeating those words until he finally grabbed the envelope from the box and look it over in its entirety before deciding to open it.

Inside was a colorful piece of paper folded up in a origami shape of a heart. One thing that his mother liked to do was make shapes out of everything that she could. It was her love of shapes that taught him his love of shapes also.

Unfolding a paper in his hand he could see the familiar handwriting that belonged to his mother.

He loved the fact that she taught him how to write and his handwriting was similar to hers. From the way that he wrote all of his Rs with a capital letter, and how he wrote his name in cursive based on what she taught him.

He took a deep breath and began to read what was written in red ink on the paper.

Now, if you are reading this letter then that means that I have finally met my demise. I have finally succumbed to my flaws and the trials and tribulations of life has finally caught up to me to claim my soul.

As you can see, I only put your name on the envelope and letter because this is how much faith that I have in you, to know that you will be the one who will take care of the affairs concerning my fate.

You have always been mama's favorite child and the one that I know I can count on in the clutch to make sure that things are going to be taken care of concerning me.

I am very grateful for the time on Earth that I was able to spend with you. You have learned so much and have put it to use to become the King that I am the most proud of.

I am very honored to be to have been your mother I am also writing this because I cannot go to my grave without telling you that the man that you have been calling your father for your whole life isn't your father. But of course, I know that you know that piece of information. However, it will come as a shock to you but Frederick has an older brother by the name of Silas DeLoach.

I was a young girl straight out of high school and I fell in love with Silas. He was good to me. Sweet, handsome, charming, and he cared for me. He wanted nothing but the best for me, but he was in love with the streets.

He couldn't focus on loving me because he was in love with the money, and in love with making sure I had the finer things. I was conflicted because he was doing what he had to do to take care of me, but it was so wrong in so many ways. I didn't know how to tell him to stop, when I was in love with the benefits that came with him being in the streets.

Long story short, Silas had ended up getting caught up in a drug raid, and was put in jail. I was there to visit him any and every chance that I could visit him. But as time went on it became evident that he was going to have to do prison time.

After a while we chose to part ways, because I didn't want to see him like that. Less than a month after he went to jail I found out I was pregnant with you.

I told him, and he told me to get in touch with his brother and meet him, and basically get to know him in a way that would get him to sleep with me. So that's what I did. And when time came to have you, I told him that you were his child instead of Silas so he went to his grave knowing that you weren't his, but raising you like his own.

I could not bear the thought of you not knowing who your father is. Your father is out of prison but has stayed away from us to respect my wishes.

He stays in Brooklyn on Nordstrom avenue.

It's not up to me to tell you to go see him. Or to encourage you to find him. I just know that you will. Because you have always been curious. You have always been the one who had to find out the solution to any problem that we faced. So I know that your inquisitive mind will not allow you to want to know as much about your father as you can.

That's all I wanted to impart on you. I pray that you forgive me for what I did in keeping this from you all this time. I have only wanted to shelter you from it all.

This is something that you will have to process and in due time, make a conscious decision as to what you want to do. I have raised you to be the smartest man and to give everyone the benefit of the doubt, so if you want to know him that's a reality that you can make happen.

I want you to know that I am here for you in spirit. You know what time it is my son. You are capable of taking this information and putting it to use to work for you.

I am confident that you will shine through the rain no matter what. I will end this for now. Hahaha. I am writing this but I know one day I will be dead and gone. I love you my baby. Everything we have gone through is not for nothing. You will be someone special one day.

"Momma Bear"

For 5 minutes after reading the letter Nouchy was mystified in total shock and disbelief because he knew exactly who Silas was. A major drug dealing kingpin in Brooklyn who had power all over the five boroughs. So to find out that this was his father was an understatement. Things had just went from sad, to totally interesting, in the five minutes that it took him to read the letter.

Having accomplished what he set out to do at the bank, he folded the paper in his pocket and told the clerk he was done. He wished the banker farewell and exited out the bank consumed by thoughts of awe and wonder.

He was headed to continue on his daily chores thinking to himself all the while, safeguard what's yours.... safeguard was yours.... and that's what he intended to do by all means whatever was necessary.... Even if it meant he would die in the process and sacrifice his life....

TO BE CONTINUED.........